ROXY

ROLLERS

ROXY

ROLLERS

JENNIFER DIANE

iUniverse, Inc.
Bloomington

ROXY ROLLERS

iUniverse books may be ordered through booksellers or by contacting:

iUniverse
1663 Liberty Drive
Bloomington, IN 47403
www.iuniverse.com
1-800-Authors (1-800-288-4677)

ISBN: 978-1-4759-7423-2 (sc)
ISBN: 978-1-4759-7424-9 (hc)
ISBN: 978-1-4759-7425-6 (e)

Library of Congress Control Number: 2013903739

Printed in the United States of America

iUniverse rev. date: 3/6/2013

~ for Leola ~

Prologue

I FIND SOCIAL EXPERIMENTS FUNNY, in a sadistic sort of way. I quite enjoy putting people into awkward positions and seeing how they react based on their learned social graces and individual internal reflex action.

So coming up with an idea like I did took extra imagination, guts, and secrecy. Most of us have seen the TV show *What Would You Do?* where scenarios, usually injustices or illegal activity—things you do not experience in everyday life—show how ordinary people react, why they react, and what they decide to do.

My mind is a little more twisted than that. It's so interesting how we would step in, step up, argue, fight for something, and even hurt the ones we love, the ones we trust the most. But with strangers, we are so afraid of offending, of hurting their feelings, of embarrassing ourselves that it gets in the way of what we have learned since before we can talk.

We even ignore those gut feelings—the ones that are there to protect our lives.

The way we have learned to behave, to treat people, and to interact with strangers is definitely a behavior learned from our parents and through school, work, TV, mentors, etc. It is also unique to where we live. Even people living in the same city will behave and react in different ways dependent on their neighborhood and social status.

So coming up with an idea like I did—well, let's just say *Primetime Live* would most definitely *not* be airing my episode, which works for me because even though my legs are quite photogenic, displaying them straight up in the air on national TV is not on my to-do list.

HBO, on the other hand… now we're talking.

I

WE STARTED SLOWLY, MAKING out using full tongues while in church, Matt grabbing my ass in the grocery store line—the basic sort of fun, childish behavior, like you did when you were a teenager making out in the basement while your parents were upstairs. The intention was to move slowly, to 'wet your whistle' so to speak. When we got married and started having babies, the opportunities slowly dwindled. I didn't ever want to be accused of being a trashy mother or anything like that, so we had to improvise. When you're stuck in the house with babies for months on end, you have to make things up to do for fun.

We started experimenting on each other, kind of our own social experiment. First we tried the basic, normal things everyone says to do when couples are bored:

"Leola, try role playing! It's so great; you can dress up like a sexy French maid, and he can be a fireman and you can—" Yeah, we can be a tacky, low-budget porn no one would ever want to watch, much less participate in. There's a reason that shit is on at one in the morning.

No thanks. So we skipped all that bullshit, didn't even bother trying it. For us, slow and steady clearly wasn't working, so we jumped right in—both bunny feet—behaving like dirty rabbits. Butt-ass naked with a fluffy tail.

Swinging. We'd never considered bringing other couples into

our relationship, but we'd both had threesomes before we were together. We've never been jealous of each other, so it wasn't really a daunting thought for us. It wasn't about love for us. It was purely about sex. Some people join the lifestyle because they're bored, and some join because they're sexual deviants and just like to have their other personality acknowledged. On both these accounts I knew we could have fun here. He got it. I got it. If you don't get it, you probably never will.

And truth be told, I've always missed playing around with girls. I'd done it through my teen years and my twenties … well, haven't we all? For all the "boys" reading this who just felt a twitch in their groins, you're not the only one. The idea of two young, naked, nubile nymphs taking out the stress of a long day by sexually disciplining each other makes a whole lot of women wetter than a New Orleans dike—pun intended.

We started out going to the swingers' clubs. We didn't know much of what to expect, so to be safe, I dressed completely slutty. I was going "all out." I mean, we've all seen videos on TV, so I felt educated enough to know my thigh-high boots, tiny skirt, and slightly see-through tank top would be a perfect fit. Days before, I took some time getting things ready for that first night, our virginity waiting in the wings. My hair took the least amount of time, tousling it with hairspray to reach the perfect messy, just-fucked look. I spent the most time on my face, as we all do when we want to look just perfect, and then realized, like I do every time, that I look better when I spend the least amount of time on my face—irony is a cruel bitch when I'm the most stressed! But of course I don't think of that until I've fucked around with my makeup so much that my green eyes are bloodshot and my face is going blotchy. I probably looked fine, but we are our own worst critics. I opted for black eyeliner, tons of mascara—*fuck the extensions*—and lip gloss to highlight my pouty lips. My outfit was waiting only because it took me the week prior to put it together.

For a mother with two kids, I was fairly and privately proud of my body, and as I admired in the mirror the length of my legs—freshly shaved and shining with a tiny hint of glitter—I felt excited to bring attention to them with my patent-leather boots. I was finally at that age where I was confident in myself to not give a shit. I'd wasted my twenties giving a shit. I was plain out of shit to give.

Matt wore jeans and a nice shirt. It's not really about the guys, anyway. *He's damn lucky I even invited him,* I thought with a laugh as I sauntered down the hall and stepped into the living room.

He whistled at me from the kitchen, where he was making us a drink, and I was impressed at how well he cleaned up. His light-brown hair was spiked up in all directions with the right amount of product without looking like a greaser, and his short-sleeved, black, button-up shirt fitted perfectly over his biceps as he involuntarily flexed while handing me a drink. The True Religions jeans cupped his ass—*oh my God, so amazing*—I just loved them on him … the man still made my thighs tingle. He was taller by only a couple inches, but we complemented each other well. *Okay, you can come.*

The first time we went it was a Friday night in the spring. The early evening was an interesting mixture of cool and warm, like the cool breeze flowing off a lake on a warm day, feeling amazing on your arms and legs, if you happen to be lucky enough to be wearing a slutty skirt. It was starting to get light out, as it does during that time of year. The extra light is a welcome sight because it's wonderful not to have to go to and from work in the dark for the next six months, but it is also a huge downfall when you live in the 'burbs and are trying to inconspicuously sneak into the family car dressed like a hooker. *Oh, hi, Sherry (my churchgoing neighbor)! *cough cough* Oh, we're just going to, um, a (spring?) costume party! *pulls down skirt to hide the front—shit!—pulled down too much, ass showing out the back* Yes, tea tomorrow sounds divine! *scrambling to get in the car without flashing your cooch to the eight-year-old boys playing street hockey* Have a great night!*

3

Insert mental note to buy a black trench coat for future excursions.

Looking back I remember we were pretty nervous despite our arrogant nature of "coolness" that we always tried to uphold. We talked a lot about what we were anticipating when we got there. We giggled like kids in Sex Ed class when the teacher said "penis." It felt good to laugh at each other, to have something alive to do again with each other. *Oh my gawd, do you think there's going to be, like, orgies going on as soon as we walk in? Do you think there'll be a pathway and a place to sit if we don't want to just jump in? Can we at least get a drink first?* I would bet everyone has those thoughts about swingers.

Two anxious newbies drove through the night following the GPS and momentarily praying the machine wouldn't flash "Swinger's Club" on the monitor—and even more, that it wouldn't save the information for the day our kids use it to go to the mall the first time on their own. We were told the building number would be on the door, but we were looking for the red light that "marks the spot." Of course, as I mentioned, it was spring, so it was still pretty light out. We had to drive slowly through this parking lot looking for numbers like a fucking pedophile driving an ice cream truck scouring the area for kids. I was just thankful no one was watching us. After finding a parking spot, we sat there for a good ten minutes. *You ready?* Nervous smiles. Deep breaths … *Fuck it. Let's go.*

As we stepped out of the van, the sounds of spring deadened with each step toward the door. Even the birds seemed to stop and watch us as we embarked on this new adventure. I could see us on a TV monitor, the world watching like we were taking the first steps on the moon.

Matt opened the door for me, and we were assaulted with low, sultry bass music. No naked sweaty bodies falling out the door. Weird. The front room was … nice. Tasteful. Black and white nude portraits on the walls. A calendar of events displaying upcoming theme parties, and mirrors strategically placed here and there. A woman about my age sitting at the desk greeted us. She was dressed in a low-cut, off-the-shoulder black top, her black hair pinned up in every direction. Her red lips smiled warmly and casually when she saw Matt and me. She was strikingly beautiful. *Are her whips and chains perhaps put away?* I hoped not too far. She was friendly as we introduced ourselves and signed in, and as our bravado heated up again, we turned and entered the mouth of the dragon's den.

2

IT WAS DARKER INSIDE—*IT is always nice to have the ugly lights dimmed*—and as our minds and eyes adjusted, we began sizing up the room. Only a few tables were occupied, a smattering of couples chatting in various corners of the intimate space. We felt eyes sizing up their competition (*why did it feel like we were lit up like a sign on Hollywood Boulevard?*) as all eyes turn to the newbies. I sucked my breath in as I summoned the small reserve of courage I had left and hung on to Matt's arm with a smile plastered on my face, praying I wouldn't trip or step awkwardly, so of course- Murphy's Law- my heel slipped out to the side.

We sauntered like a couple of pros over to the bar area, which was really just a modern kitchen, to pour some liquid courage—*make mine a double!*—and lingered there, anticipating walking into the open area to find a table.

A woman casually floated over while we were mixing our drinks and nodded a soft hello. With slow motion she brushed past me, caressing my arm as she reached for a straw. My breath caught. I felt myself stop for a moment, surprised at my body's natural reaction to the closeness of a woman like that. *I liked that ... yes ...I remember how I really like that ...* I smiled at her and slowly turned around, stepping closer to Matt. I leaned over and whispered in his ear, "I think I like it here." He reflected on my words, and I instinctively knew what he was thinking: *Girl on girl? Yes, please.*

We found a table off to the side that gave us a good vantage point of most of that main floor. In front of us to the right was the dance floor, flanked by two stripper poles, one on each corner. Of course the obligatory disco ball hovered over the dance floor in the middle of the room, and it was so much more overt here; it belonged so much that it stood out in a strange, obvious kind of way. The dance floor was small, about the size of a space you'd get if you tried to squeeze a dance floor into a large living room at a house party. Mirrors hung in the two corners behind the stripper poles to ensure you got a good view on all angles, and the disco ball spun slowly, teasing and winking at itself, on and on forever.

About fifteen tables of various sizes and heights surrounded the dance floor. Behind them, just in front of the mirrors, were a couple of couches facing each other, a coffee table in the center for a quaint visit. Picture a men's club occupied by cigars and scotch. The couches were dark red, soft velvet. They almost looked like they belonged in a Victorian brothel, sexy and firm ... worn out in all the right places. Abstract pictures covered the walls, showing off their design, mostly black and white, surrounding the room. The kitchen area was supplied with soda and ice, glasses, lemons and limes, straws, stemware, and shot glasses, and guests were expected to bring their own booze, as we had. A pantry with shelves full of liquor marked with their owners' name was neighbored by a restaurant-style fridge with glass doors, and it too was full of booze. To our left was a hallway, and behind us was the door to the front room and to the outside. It was nice, tasteful, dark, and sexy but comfortable. I couldn't wait to get this party started.

We didn't say too much to each other as we sat there those first few minutes. It was a smorgasbord of sights and sounds, not to mention the emotional impact of what we were getting ourselves into. We made small talk with each other, too overwhelmed and distracted for a real conversation. Matt reflected he thought it would be busier, and I nodded and sipped my drink in agreement, hoping I didn't dress up for nothing.

After a few minutes a man came over and introduced himself to us as Tim. He was Candy's husband, the girl who had greeted us in the front room, and they were the owners of the establishment. He was going to show us around, if we'd like.

Tim was a good-looking guy, kind of classic good looks; Dirty blond hair, with not one out of place. He was tall, thin with an angular build and he sported a nice dress shirt, nice jeans, and nice shoes. A firm handshake for Matt. Nice, warm, enveloping hug and a polite kiss for me. Nothing like what I would ever be interested in. Pleasant enough guy, just too boring-good-looking for me. It may sound rude, but it feels as if people like that just wouldn't have much going for them personality-wise, you know? Like they never went through adversity in their lives, probably had a perfect childhood, played football, dated girls here and there without a problem, really. Probably was the one who did the breaking up. Good-looking guys like that don't get dumped.

Guys like that don't get by my walls. I need some depth, some hurt, some brokenness somewhere in my man. How horrible does that sound? But you know what I mean. I need something to grip on to. First of all, speaking generally, girls need "projects" or we get bored. And second, we need to feel some kind of motherly superiority with our man. Without these two ingredients, you get a Howdy Doody guy. I like bad boys, but I also like men who cry. I like men who *need* me. I like to fantasize that my man would crumble without me. That being said, it *has* to be balanced with the *I-don't-give-a-fuck* guy. The *I'm-an-asshole* guy. The *I'm-gonna-bust-some-shit-up* guy. And the ever important *I'm-gonna-fuck-you-sideways-till-tomorrow* guy. I'm a cliché. Yeah, Tim was all right. Just like a puppy. Fun to play with, but they'll love anyone who waves a treat in front of them. My treat likes a bigger kind of pooch.

Tim took us around and showed us the coat check and the main room, and then he took us down the hall—*the* hall, the dark, where-do-you-think-*that*-one-leads-to hall. Turned out to be a short walk, but it was just not very well lit, so from where we were sitting it looked to be a lot longer. Down this hallway to the left were the bathrooms, complete with wipes, mirrors, condoms, and hand sanitizer. *They think of everything.*

The door on the left was the playroom.

Visions of orgies filled my head. *This is where everyone is!* Blindfolded virgins, masked men from foreign lands, gasps, cries, and pleasures filled with submissive whispers. *Let me at 'em!*

The door was open. I peeked around the corner and waited for my body to follow. Instead, I ended up looking like a ten-year-old boy trying to sneak a peek into the girls' locker room. Sadly, the room seemed to be vacant.

My hopes and dreams fell away like the last remnants of a dried-up waterfall. *Where the fuck is all the sex? Where's all the wet and sucking and licking? Why is no one fornicating in the name of some pagan god?* Disappointment and relief dueled aggressively, and I was fascinated that I wasn't sure of the victor.

Tim took us in the vacant room and asked us if we'd seen a playroom before. *Nooo …* His face revealed something, but I couldn't tell if he was disappointed that we were inexperienced or thrilled that he got to take our playroom-explanation virginity.

To our left was a large pleather mattress, large enough for four to six people to enjoy together. Spirits of orgies past flickered in my mind's eye. In the middle of the room was a large swing. I'm pretty worldly, but I'd never seen a swing in real life before, so it was hard to tell what it was without anyone in it. In the back corner was a smaller, rectangular pleather mattress, more the size for two people. In the back to our right was a curtained-off section, where Tim took us to show a couch facing a TV quietly playing porn all night.

At all "stations" were baby wipes, condoms, and paper towels. *Handy!* Back into the room in the last corner was a large, person-sized cross right out of Pontius Pilate's playground. It was flanked by a small table with a black whip. *Interesting… should I be turned on or mortified…?*

We left the room and went back to our table. I asked Tim about the lack of bodies there, and he explained that most people don't come until after ten or even eleven at night. Made sense. Apparently, everyone's had the same "'burbs experience," so they leave like vampires in the night, flying off to bite holes in their virtue, drinking the blood of their souls until they fell into ecstasy.

Our first night at the club was disappointingly uneventful. We danced, we watched, and we talked. We met a few people, and still we danced and talked. A lot. We did not go into the playroom. We watched sexy girls dancing on the poles. We watched unattractive women dancing on the poles. We touched and laughed and drank everything in.

Then we went home and fucked like two jailed lovers on a conjugal visit.

3

WHEN MATT AND I first started out, we laid down some ground rules, communication being the most important part. Cheating doesn't work because of the lying, the deceit, the sneaking around, etc. We all know why cheating doesn't work. This was a venture for both of us to enter together, not for one or the other to enjoy on their own, so we sat up one night and established the general rules and pointed out that the rules will change as time goes on.

Matt slowly poured me a second glass of wine. He smiled, and I could see the little hamster on the wheel turning, turning, and gaining speed. I waited, knowing he was thinking something fun, a crossing the line kind of fun. "Okay, I'm thinking." He paused for effect. "How far are we talking here?" He handed me my glass and sat across from me at the kitchen table. It was the morning after our first night at the club, and we were still riding high on the fumes of what was left over.

"Well, why don't we do it in stages…? Oh! I know. Let's start from the head and work our way down?"

He locked my eyes. "I'm listening…"

I took a sip of my wine. "Well, let's only do things that involve our faces the first couple of times we go. Kissing only."

He reached across the table and slowly walked his fingers up my arm. "And then we move down to include the chest area?"

"Yes, chest and head, and the more times we go, we move down the body to include more and more as we get comfortable."

His fingers stopped walking and he pulled back. "And then… we…"

"Yes." I smiled at him. He looked at me. I leaned over and kissed him. "It will be so fun, babe. We just need to make sure we talk to each other. We might be at the head for six visits, and that's okay. You might want to go to chest in two visits, but I want to stay at head. Or vice versa. We need to respect each other."

"I agree," he said. "No pressure. If one of us isn't ready, we wait. This isn't a race, right?"

"Exactly. This is for both of us. This is for fun!" I sat back and thought. "If we do this right, we could redefine relationships…"

"Don't get your hopes up. There are way too many people in this world to convert. If they can't do it with religion, you won't do it with sex." He laughed.

I smiled and looked down. Sometimes he thinks he's pretty funny.

But I am always up for a challenge…

Matt and I moved at a steady pace. We went to the clubs about once a month. The body game worked pretty well—like ocean surf on the shore. The tide went in and out; sometimes there were waves, but for the most part just beauty in the moonlight. I felt like we were dancing. Sometimes we did some salsa, sometimes the waltz, and even a few break dances, but it was beautiful nonetheless. Our relationship grew, our securities fastened, our emotions cradled in the firmest branch. No bow would break here. We made friends, we had fun, and we kept our relationship exciting. It was nice to make love to my husband, and he was finally opening up to some hardcore fucking.

And then—

We got bored. Ha! What a cruel joke! What more do people have to do to keep their relationships from going stale? I am *not* going to play Bingo!

One night we went to the club expecting nothing new. Now,

for the most part, everyone in the lifestyle is respectful of each other. When new people come to the club, you can spot them a mile away. They might as well have a spotlight on them with a neon sign flashing 'We Are Newbies and We Are Terrified!' A newbie is a lifestyle virgin. I remember the feeling too. You can almost *feel* the spotlight and neon sign on you. It was so awful. Matt and I almost always went over to talk to newbies because we couldn't bear to have these poor people sit by themselves—the awkwardness almost tangible, like snakes slithering in and out of their arms and legs and resting on the table waiting for the slightest move to strike. But it's also so great meeting new people who are open to this kind of thing.

So this one night, as we walked over to this new couple, I couldn't help thinking, *This is going to be the saaaaame thing, the saaaame conversation, the saaaame outcome.*

The couple looked over at us, a mix of fear and anticipation on their faces.

"Hi there!" Matt shook the guy's hand and then the girl's. "I'm Matt, and this is my wife, Leola."

"Hi! Steve and Emma," Steve said. We all shook hands.

"Can we sit with you guys?" I asked. I looked at them both, trying to get a reading. They looked at each other and back at us. Steve caught my eye, and for a moment there, I felt a connection that caught me off guard. Almost a déjà vu.

"Sure!" they said in unison.

We pulled a couple of stools over and put down our drinks. "We've never seen you guys here before. Is it your first time?" Matt smiled to put them at ease.

"Is it *that* obvious?" Emma asked, laughing. "We thought we were doing pretty good."

"No not at all, you just look like you're watching the execution of a puppy," Matt teased.

We all laughed.

"It's all good; we're just giving you a hard time. We were new once too." It was easy, relaxed.

Steve purposely caught my eye again, and I felt a small spark.

What was that? It felt ... good. I looked guiltily over at Matt. What was happening?

Matt was sitting right there; I wasn't doing anything wrong...

The four of us talked and laughed all night. We said hi to our regular friends there but didn't leave Steve and Emma's table all night except when Emma and I danced and when the boys refilled our drinks. Wow, she was so sexy. We dirty-danced together, heels, legs, and arms tangled in a musical frenzy. I kissed her, and she kissed me back firmly, tenderly, enticingly. My body responded, grounded in its reaction. I felt myself drawn to her so strongly, more than I had with any other girl. My brain split in two, and as the two halves spoke to each other, I pulled away, holding up a finger for to her to wait a moment and went over to my husband.

I whispered in his ear and asked him something I'd never asked before: "Can I take her to the playroom for a few minutes? Maybe in a few minutes you and Steve can come and watch? I just want to have some fun with her—just us."

As I pulled away from Matt, he squeezed my arm and smiled. He nodded.

I turned back to Emma and asked her to join me, and she looked at Steve for a moment. She quickly nodded at me, and we flew off together down the hall like ghosts through a cloud.

I was the first one in the still-empty room and led Emma to the smaller pleather mattress in the corner. As I crawled backward on top of it, I pulled Emma to me, our lips locked, and our hands found each other's thighs and waist as we pulled each other closer. She was so soft, her full lips perfectly complementing mine, our tongues synchronizing their dance, wet and firm as they explored. My heart raced, her body was so beautiful.

Emma took the lead then, pushing me gently on to my back, our lips never losing their embrace. I bit her softly and pulled on her lip, her warm breath falling on me like glitter while she deliberately ran her fingers up my shaking thighs, smooth and silky under her velvet hands, where she found me already wet and waiting for her. We breathed in each other's scent and locked eyes in the dimly lit room, her hand and fingers moving inside my panties, my hips raised up to meet her halfway.

I couldn't wait the extra nanosecond for her to cross the distance on her own. My pussy was pulsing, throbbing, soaking wet, and I grabbed her wrist to make her touch me harder. I turned my face to her neck, and she pulled her hair over to bare it for me, so soft, and she smelled incredible. Her earlobe flirted against my face, and I sucked and bit as I concentrated on guiding her hand to exactly where I wanted it to be. I felt her breath quicken, her body harden. She was trying to hold back, if only to make this last longer. I never wanted this to end.

She pulled away to guide my panties off slowly, teasingly (*chastity belt not required here!*). Her fingers softly entered me—*too fucking soft*—and I pressed against her, rising up to force her deeper, and she finally pushed hard inside, and I grabbed her around her ass, her sweet, tight, full ass pillowing under as my fingers dug in, and the want and need inside me grew, and the testosterone took over and I willed myself to grow a cock so I could pound her into the bed.

As I pulled my face out of her neck to find her nipples, I saw two figures in the room off to the side, but I quickly dismissed them. Nothing else existed at this moment.

I quickly pulled her top off over her head, needing her hand to not break rhythm, and expertly unclasped her bra with my other. My mouth found her nipples, erect and soft, like a strawberry on top of a mound of ice cream, and I touched one first with my tongue before her breast and nipple filled my mouth. I sucked with deep desire.

Her fingers worked furiously on my clit and inside my soaking wet pussy, and I pulled back my mouth to bite her nipple. She cried out, and with her free hand she pulled my head back using a fistful of my hair. She crushed my lips with hers and suddenly pulled her hand out of me, making me cry out in need and want.

I pulled my mouth away, breaking the suction of her lips and pushed her down to finish me off, and I felt myself cry out when her lips touched my throbbing clit. I bucked and trembled as she licked and sucked my clit, so hard and sensitive by that time. Up and down her tongue worked, nibbling and sucking, my clit full and throbbing with every movement of her tongue. My hips ground up and down to match her tongue. Her fingers were up so far inside me, I felt her rubbing my G-spot, and my back arched and I ground into her fingers, feeling the warmth build, but I couldn't wait any longer. It took only moments before I came, her fingers and tongue working expertly together, synchronized in their movements. She drank my cum as it poured out of me like hot lava, and I cried out and held her head, squeezing in the intensity of my orgasm. Knowing she wasn't going to last much longer, she finished quickly but gently, knowing my clit was raw and sensitive, and she laid back, spreading her legs before me, her skirt already pulled up, revealing her smooth, wet pussy.

As if we had previously choreographed this, I eagerly went down on her, my hands taking her hips, and I drank from her like a golden cup of nectar from the gods, created only for me to drink. She was warm, sweet and soft, hairless; she felt like liquid silk. My tongue memorized every crevice of her pussy, every fold, every mound. Her hands caressed my head, entangling my hair in her fingers, squeezing and pulling. Her clit stood at attention, begging to be flicked, and as my tongue and mouth sucked and fucked, her hips moved in rhythm with me. She bucked faster and faster as I sucked harder and harder and fucked her deeper and deeper with my fingers, her thighs shaking against my head, her hands furiously pulling my hair until she cried out. I fed like a vampire feeding and sucking the blood of a lover.

We collapsed, and the room around us slowly came back to reality. I noticed one item at a time until our husbands came into view—first Steve, who had found his way to Emma's head opposite me, and then Matt, who was grabbing me from behind.

I stood up and turned to him and felt his hard cock against me. I unbuckled his pants and sat with my legs spread, still dripping pussy juice down my inner thigh, and he didn't wait for me to guide him in. I only had a moment to wrap my legs around his back when he entered me hard, his arms wrapped around my back, and he took me right there, hard and furious, pounding me into the bed.

Steve and Emma melted away in the background, presumably mirroring our efforts. Matt fucked me hard, without thought, without romance, without a care. Primal and raw, my husband took me for himself until he cried out only moments later, clinging to me in mad passion, filling me with his cum, his hard cock pulsing inside me as he filled me with everything he had.

Once Emma and I were cleaned up, we joined the party going in full force in the main room. Steve and Matt left the room looking relatively the same as when they'd entered—*unfair!*—to get us ladies a drink.

We met them at our table *quite a few* minutes later, permanent grins displayed proudly on all our faces. Trying to go on with the evening on a normal note proved to be challenging, as it was our first encounter with the playroom—and last, I should add—but after a couple of drinks, things settled back to normal. Normal, however, was not what this was turning out to be with this couple.

At some point, Steve asked me to dance. He took me in his arms and held me firmly against him and talked softly into my neck. Small talk mostly, fun, light quips about what had just happened. But he held me close, like I had been there before, his arms so strong. When he looked in my eyes, he drank me in like I was the elixir that kept him alive. It was uncomfortable and seductive at the same time. I felt as if I should pull away but couldn't move. My body felt like it was taking over my mind. There was something there...

Matt danced with Emma on the other side of the small dance floor, only a couple of dancers between us. They were laughing; we were all having such a good night.

This is different. Dark thoughts formed in my mind. *Let's do something different ... I want something different.* I started to quiver. I felt like I was floating. *Yes, we can do this.* I felt my eyes fill with hunger. *We will do this.*

The warm stirring filled me. Now I just had to find a way to present it to Matt. I looked back at him. I had a feeling it wouldn't be too hard a sell. I turned my face back to Steve. I felt him move and I smiled. He held me tighter. I had a feeling it wouldn't be too hard a sell for Steve, either.

4

MATT WOKE UP JUST before I did, and I felt him stretch and sit up on his side of the bed to turn off the alarm so it wouldn't wake me. His back was to me. I loved his back. The wide strength of a man's back is so sexy, and his was by all definitions damn perfect. His back was tattooed, which makes it doubly hot for me. He has skulls and scorpions of the right side and a tribal mask on the left. On the back of each arm are the names of our children Charlie and Heather. He was a strong man. A man's man, if you know what I mean. Hands rough enough to chop wood and build forts. Hands soft enough to touch me with tenderness, a combination that drives me wild.

He looked back at me to see if I was still sleeping. "Morning, beautiful." He leaned over and kissed me. We lay like that for a quiet moment, and then he got up to get ready for work.

When I woke again at six forty-five the sun was just starting to light up the room. Matt's side of the bed was empty; I hadn't even heard him leave. I stretched the beautiful, long, glorious stretch of a cat, looked out the window, and contemplated going back to sleep. For a while I lay there thinking of the day ahead. *Not much on the agenda today,* I thought happily. I lowered my hands and they found their sweet, warm friend, and they exchanged wet, warm pleasantries. My hands worked furiously and expertly until I cried out as silently as I could and then turned over, reset the alarm for seven thirty, and closed my eyes. The kids could start getting ready without me today, I thought. And I promptly fell back asleep.

I was greeted with sunshine when I woke up the third time, so I put on my housecoat and went downstairs. The kids were in the kitchen eating breakfast and watching cartoons.

I breezed into the kitchen and announced, "Good morning!"

They looked up. "Morning, Mom!" They both said.

I kissed their heads as I walked past them. It was radiant in the kitchen; the windows faced east, and the morning sun glowed orange and warm in the heart of my house, so fresh and bright and full of possibilities.

I made their lunches while they ate. Heather was nine and had long blonde hair, her bangs clipped over to the side this morning, framing her face. Charlie was thirteen with sandy-brown hair chopped all over, thick wisps sticking out this way and that.

They were good kids, and I really enjoyed being their mom.

"Hey, Mom, can I go over to Scott's after school today? We just want to hang and practice." Charlie and his friends were keen on getting a band going. He'd been playing guitar for only six months, but between texting and sleeping, he was getting pretty good.

"Sure, sweetie. Remember homework first," I reminded him.

"Ummm hmmm," he mumbled. We both knew he'd cram it in on Sunday night, as usual. But he did all right in school, so I couldn't complain.

"Mommy?"

"Yes, my girl?" I put too much mustard on the sandwich and wiped it off into the sink.

"Did you finish my poodle skirt for the dance?" She didn't look away from the TV. "Almost. I'll finish it today, okay?"

"Okay," she said.

I finished preparing their lunches and put the kettle on for a nice cup of tea. Then I grabbed the remote and turned on the morning news.

"*Hey!*" They protested.

I smiled and got my tea ready. "Cartoons rot your brains. Wouldn't you like to see what the weather is going to be like later in the day? To see what's happening in the world around you?"

They replied with grunts and groans and sure's and whatever's.

I chose green tea and peppermint for this morning's combination. I love tea and the news in the morning. God I'm getting old.

As the kids put their dishes in the sink and grabbed their bags, I let the tea steep and went to help with coats and backpacks. I was looking forward to my day off. Time for me to think, get things done, do nothing. It didn't matter. It was my day.

"Bye, Mom!" I got a kiss from Heather, but of course Charlie was too cool for that sort of thing. An absentminded wave was his good–bye, and they were gone.

Deep breath. Silence. Sweet, beautiful silence. I smiled as I walked back to the kitchen, my arms hugging my chest. This was going to be a great morning.

Bling! I unplugged the charger from my cell and checked my texts. There was one from Matt. *Hey, babe. Hope you had a good sleep. You up for something fun tonight??*

I smiled. *Always. Do you mean what I think you mean? I've been waiting for you to be ready.*

I'd been feeling impatient lately, but Matt always comes around in his own time. I've learned over the years to not force him. It's no fun when I have to force him. Last weekend I tried something new, a subtle suggestion. It was a change from my normal routine of tantrums or taking advantage of him sexually. Sometimes that triggers the beast in him to come out and play.

Bling! I read the text. *Thank you for waiting, babe. I am ready.*

I felt the familiar rush building, the hunger, the warmth spreading through me like a waterfall and a volcano erupting together, warm and wet, dark and clear. *Finally,* I thought. I texted, *You are my love, always. I will find a sleepover for Heather tonight. xo*

I put down the phone and drank my tea.

5

THE THING IS THIS: we didn't set out to hurt anyone, least of all ourselves; it is only out of morbid curiosity that I came up with this idea in the first place. That being said, it didn't take much convincing for Matt to go along with it. We mostly had to convince ourselves that we weren't evil people.

And of course, like many plans, it was a simple one. Straightforward, uncomplicated, basic. In. Out. Really: a blip on the radar.

But most importantly, it was going to be fucking fun.

Matt and I had a small, tight group of friends, where most of us have been friends since college, and our children have grown up together. We have a few new friends, through work friends' friends, stuff like that. In life, you meet people along the way you naturally gravitate toward, and through common interests, convenience, and simple gravitational pull you create a safe place for you and your family to journey through life with.

I have great support from friends. My longest friendship is Samantha, from high school. We were best friends into our early twenties, and then she moved away when she went to school and met her husband. We've always remained best friends even though we only see each other once a year or so. I have a couple of friends I'm closer to than others, but I couldn't separate them into one best friend or another.

Except for Ever. Ever is my best friend, my conscience, my

heart, and my rock. We met a few years ago through her husband, Clint, who's a welder. He was working at some welder's shop, where Matt was trying to sell one of the commercial properties in the same building. One afternoon Clint's truck wouldn't start, and Matt helped boost it. They started talking and Matt, who is notorious for bringing home strays, invited him and his wife to join us for drinks that night. I immediately fell in love with Ever, and we've been inseparable ever since.

Ever is everything I want to be when I grow up. She is the same age as me and has bleached blonde spiky hair, too many ear piercings, a bunch of tattoos, and doesn't give a shit about anything or anybody. She has a trucker's vocabulary and makes sure her nails and makeup are loud and proud. Her parents are hard core hippies, as you can tell by her name, but she is everything but. She treats her husband like a god even though he's a tool—*my opinion, of course*—and tells everyone else to go fuck themselves on a regular basis.

Matt and Clint clicked in the let's-all-hang–out-every-once-in-a-while kind of way, but they don't hang out on their own. Clint is an overweight, chain-smoking, beer–swilling, typical blue-collared man who doesn't do much after work but sit on the couch and burp, nothing interesting to bring to the table for any conversation. It eludes any stretch of the imagination how Ever found and still finds him attractive; I think she still sees him through rose-colored glasses, still sees the cool twenty-five-year-old she fell in love with. The problem is that twenty-five-year-old "cool" guys like that turn into forty-year-olds who have nothing going for them anymore.

It's hard to believe because Ever is *so* amazing. I see men fall over themselves when she walks into a room, but she seems oblivious. It's like watching people running for money falling from the sky, pushing each other out of the way, stepping on heads, and running into each other. Whenever we go out, I make her wait outside so I can find a table and get situated in the direction of the door, so when she walks in, I can watch the men's faces. She walks in like she owns the place, and I fall harder for her every time. It's the best part of the night for me.

It was killing me to keep such a secret, and I needed a girlfriend to tell it to. But I'm afraid she— whoever I told—would find it *way* too much to handle; she would look at Matt and me in a completely different manner, and nothing would be the same. *I'm dying over here.*

Our friends are by no means prudes, but I recognized that had I not personally come up with this insane idea, if I was to have heard close friends of mine were doing this, it might've made me uncomfortable around them, the very least of which I wouldn't feel safe leaving my husband in her company no matter how close friends we all may have been.

I fought with myself for hours that morning, and the debate got heated. Do I tell Ever my plan, or do I wait to tell her once it's started? I didn't want her to talk me out of it, but on the other hand, would I be able to go through with it without being able to verbally assault her with every detail for fear of imploding?

I violently cleaned the house, arguing with the vacuum, physically abusing the dust rag, and drowning the bathtub in frustration. Ever knew of Matt's and my involvement in the lifestyle, and she had no problem with it, even came with us one night to try it out. Funny enough, for how much I find Ever physically attractive and our emotional bond strong, we did not cross the line at the club.

My heart cracked slightly when she danced with another woman to Nine Inch Nail's "Closer," and we stood close and proclaimed our love for each other in a drunken confessional, but even in that stupor, we didn't "go there" with each other. Nor with each other's husband (*gross*).

I thought about this as I took the rug from the front hall to beat the shit out of it outside (*bad rug!*). With that being said, I rationalized, she would be cool with my idea, and I managed to justify my decision. And I gently put the rug back as if it was my decision personified, and I was afraid of upsetting it and changing its mind and called Ever before I could chicken out.

She answered on the first ring. "Morning, darling," she dripped in enthusiasm. (*Good! She was in a good mood!*)

"Hey, you. What're you up to?" I asked.

"Cleaning. You?"

"Same. Wanna blow this popsicle stand and go sit on a patio?" I asked, holding my breath.

"You fucking *know* it! I can be ready in thirty minutes out the door. I'll quickly tidy the rest of this shit so it looks like I gave a flying fuck and meet you there," she spat out, knowing "there" was The CupBored in Comfort, the most central place between our two houses, where we always meet up.

"Fuckin A!" I yelled back, laughing, and hung up. And then threw up. No, just kidding. I quickly scanned the main rooms, turned on the dishwasher, and went to finish our room, knowing thirty minutes meant at least forty-five. But that was okay; I needed the extra few minutes to gather my thoughts.

She was there before me, waiting at a table on the patio sprinkled in shade from one of the trees that surrounded the pub. She must've really not wanted to finish cleaning today, and I didn't blame her. It was finally nice enough out where the wind didn't carry that winter bite to it.

She stood up to hug me, and the waitress came around us with the drinks Ever had already ordered.

"Turns out I don't need thirty minutes to finish cleaning when I couldn't care less!" She laughed. "As if Clint gives a shit anyway." She winked at me as she took a sip on her straw.

"Ya think?" I laughed. "So. I want to talk to you," I started. Ever and I don't beat around the bush. Let's Get This Shit Done is our motto. I picked up my glass to wet my whistle.

"All right. I'm ready." She leaned back in her chair with her drink in her hand, and waited.

I leaned forward, elbows on the table, and stirred my drink.

I started to draw a blank. The pub patio was empty except for us and one other group of three on the other side. The music came out the open doors of the pub at a perfect volume, and the wind was slight so as not to carry my voice too far to our neighboring pub patrons engaged in some deep conversation of their own.

I smiled and started. "So, you know Matt and I are in the lifestyle, and you know how I told you we're getting pretty bored of it."

She nodded.

"Well." I paused. "I've come up with a crazy idea and I want to run it by you. Not asking for permission, but I'm going to need to dump verbal diarrhea on you from time to time."

"Okay, that's cool," she said. "Tell me."

"Okay. So." I took a sip, and then the waitress came over and—*yes please we need another drink*—she whipped back inside.

"Now, remember that you love me and you know me and you trust me and what I'm going to tell you—if you never want to hear about it again just tell me—but you still have to love me and we'll just pretend Matt and I aren't doing anything that could jeopardize our friend—"

"Oh holy shit, just fucking tell me already," Ever butted in. "Come on!" she pushed when I paused, looking at her like a scared little kid. "Out with it!"

"Okay. I was thinking…"

When the kids got home from school I was in the best mood. I'd had "two enthusiastic thumbs up" from Ever, and the kids and I talked about the plans for the weekend. Heather was going to sleep over at Jenna's for the night, and Charlie asked if he could stay at Scott's, if that was okay. They wanted to watch super scary movies until the wee hours of the morning. After all the kinks were worked out, we made plans to go to a movie Saturday afternoon. Saturday night the kids planned to invite a couple friends over for a fire in the backyard. It would be the first of the year now that the snow had melted and it was supposed to be a mild weekend. And of course on Sunday, chores and laundry needed to be done.

After a late lunch/early supper on Friday, the kids cleared the table while I cleaned up the kitchen. Then Heather and Charlie left to get their things together for their sleepovers.

As I cleaned I tried to put together different scenarios. I was so filled with anticipation I didn't even hear Charlie reenter the kitchen.

"Why are you smiling like that, Mom?" Charlie looked at me with curious suspicion.

I snapped out of my reverie. "I just love my life, Charlie. Do you know that? I'm very lucky."

He looked at me like I was ninety years old and had really nothing left to live for. He shrugged. "All righty, then. Am I okay to go?"

I smiled at my boy; it was fun being a teenager who knew everything. Those were some good times. "You're good to go! Love you, and be good!"

He turned, no kiss of course—"Love you, too"—and grabbed his bag and left.

I went upstairs to help Heather get her things together. I showed her the newly finished poodle skirt, and she shrieked with glee at my "professional" job.

After the usual *"I forgot my _____!"* seven times, we were out the door and drove the three minutes to her friend Jenna's house.

I knocked on the door and Jenna's dad answered. "Hi, Heather!" he said. "Hey, Leola." Sam was a big guy; kind of the beer-belly biker look without the tattoos and long hair. Actually, more the mountain-man look, scruffy face, big everything. I'd always had a secret crush on him. He looked like he could pick you up and put you in your place.

"Hey, Sam." I smiled and looked down. Remembering Heather as she rushed past us, I looked up again. "Thanks for letting Heather come for a sleepover. Uh, she's been wanting to play rock band with Jenna again." *I'm so dumb. What am I? Fifteen? Sheesh.* The sexual tension was palpable. Sam was married—I don't know if happily—but that's a moot point really. It's not like we'd ever do anything; our daughters were best friends.

"I'll call in the morning and see how she is. We're going to a movie in the afternoon, so I need to pick her up by two at the latest, unless you need me to come get her before that."

Sam scratched his arm. "No plans for us; that sounds good."

I smiled a little and turned to go. "Okay. Have a good night. See you tomorrow." Such a dork.

All right, home to set some plans in motion.

6

MY HUSBAND IS AN asshole.

Matt is hot. I'm talking all-around hot: on personality; on good-dad brownie points; on making me feel special, sexy, important, everything hot. Wicked job hot. I don't quite know how I landed this package, but I did. Perhaps I had some good karma stored up from my past life and I am now cashing in on the life lottery. I don't know. I don't question it, I'm just thankful for it.

I don't deserve him. Of that I'm sure. I don't appreciate him as much as I should. I try but fall pretty short sometimes. And as we all know, women need a balance of an asshole somewhere in there. Otherwise we lose interest. It is the unfortunate secret we girls keep and don't quite know how to articulate to men. But it's the truth. We need an asshole somewhere. As much as men need a challenge or they lose interest, so do women.

This is where my husband is an asshole. Let me take you on a tour. We've been married fifteen years. Children. House. Blah blah blah. There's something wrong with me in the sense that I don't want the picket-fence life. It bores the fuck out of me. I like to have my cake and eat it too. I don't see why it's okay for guys to have all the fucking perks in life and why we women have to understand this about men and give them grace and all that shit. Fuck that. I am a woman, and men can bloody well understand and give *me* grace.

Now understand this: I appreciate the feminist movement. However, I feel a few things got lost in the mix somewhere. First, I like pink. I think it's wrong to teach our girls that it's wrong to like pink and that it's wrong to like to have and play with babies. Women are women for a reason. We are soft, we are beautiful, we are nurturing, and we are better at a lot of things men are just not and *it's okay to celebrate these differences and appreciate them.*

Second, I think men *should* open our doors and treat us to dinner and learn from our grandfathers before it's gone forever that being a gallant man is a lost art and that truly appreciating women for *being* a woman is on the extinction list, and for that I am sad.

My husband was raised by a feminist. This is not a bad thing, and like I said, I truly appreciate what the feminist movement did for us women. I just feel the pendulum needs to swing back a little. We are not equal; women are just better at a lot of things men aren't. And this is okay. Where my husband is an asshole is that he was never taught the gallant skills of our grandfathers. Even though I am fully capable of doing everything myself, I don't want to. Sometimes I want to be swept off my feet.

And sometimes I want to be fucked by a man's man. You know what I mean? I want to be seriously *fucked.* Sideways and backwards. Picked-up-and-put-in-my-place *fucked.*

My husband—before the lifestyle, I should clarify—was more of a lover. And while I love that and wouldn't trade it in for the world, I *do* need more. And I have tried to get him to do more. It is only every so often when I stamp my feet enough that I get what I want. He digs his heels in a lot, though. He really makes me fight for it. I fucking love that. He teases me with it. It makes me really hot for him when he does that.

And then… I want more. That's when I come up with the best ideas to fuck someone up.

7

RELATIONSHIP A CONNECTION, ASSOCIATION, or involvement; a connection between persons by blood or marriage; or a sexual involvement; affair.

Relationships are funny. They are as important as breathing, eating, and sleeping. I believe no one can live without a relationship, not even hermits. They have relationships with the land, with the trees … with the solitude too, if we want to get technical.

Now, there are some people who can mate for life. There are friendships that last for a reason, a season, and a lifetime. There are the parent-child relationships that last forever (some don't). Work relationships, spiritual relationships. The list is endless, really.

Marriages are the most scrutinized, rule-enforced relationships I can think of. My parents have a great relationship. A little rough at the beginning, mind you, but great now. They split up for a time when I was a teenager. It was a rough time for my dad; he'd lost his dad to cancer, and back in the '70s you didn't talk much about your problems, especially men, so my dad turned to drinking. He left for a while, which in hindsight was probably the best. I saw him very drunk only a couple of times when my brother and I stayed with him, but for the most part he was good during our visits. He still drank but did not get obliterated. It was scary to see him really drunk. He wasn't an angry drunk, he was a crying, pathetic drunk. It was awful.

My mom went on a few dates during this time. It was weird to see her going out with other men. My brother is five years younger than me, so he would be in bed by the time she went out. But I always thought how interesting it was that she still loved my dad but would go out with other men. *Do you love my dad or not?* She was so timid though, always home early, only went out with the same guy a few times and kept it light, that kind of thing.

My father still came over for dinner sometimes, and everything felt normal when he was around. My mother would hug him on her way to the table, laugh at his jokes, and cry only when he headed back to his apartment. It was hard, but I think now it was good for him to feel that true friendship with her. She never let him down; she was always there for him at the drop of a hat. He was wrestling with his demons, and it was more protection for my brother and me to not see our father like that on a daily basis. She didn't want us to be disgusted by him. That's what she told me years later. Now I am old enough to appreciate what she did, and I thanked her for it.

When I was sixteen, he sobered up, and my parents moved in a healthier direction. My father started talking more and drinking less. He was at our house more than he was at his own, and my mother eventually invited him to move back home. The time he was gone was like a blip. When I think back now, with as much as he was around it felt as if he'd only been gone a short time. My parents' relationship since then has been something I've always looked up to. They are still so much in love.

I've often wondered over the years how my mom could love my dad and cry when he left and want him to move back and be with us but go out on dates with other men.

I just feel that it was how I was raised for a bit there and nothing bad happened to any of us. I didn't love my mother any less. He didn't love her any less. She was open and honest about it. She was not deceitful; she was not sneaking around or lying. And I think if I'd told her it bothered me, she would have stopped. She just needed to feel important to another man.

Ahhh… we all justify our wants in whatever way makes the most sense so we can get away with it.

I think I've never felt normal about relationships. Sometimes I feel like a bull in a china shop. I just don't belong and feel see-through sometimes. Like if anyone was to look hard enough, he or she could see right through my facade, of trying to maintain this picket-fence family, the *Leave it to Beaver* mom, the playboy wife, the Mary Tyler Moore working woman. Does nobody but me feel exhausted? Sometimes I feel like yelling at random people as they walk by on the street, their tunnel vision blinding them from what's around the corner. Is this what it's *really* all about? Keeping up with the Joneses for*ever*?

I can't be the only person who feels this way.

So, relationships. Marriage. I think that as much as we want to feel this natural attraction to one person and have it last for eighty-whatever years, it's just not realistic. It's like telling a kid to be quiet for two hours during a circus show. It would be impossible. Can it be done? Of course. *Anything* can be done, but to expect this from every child is just not feasible. So for adults to stay 100 percent faithful for eighty years with one person is equally as difficult. For sure it *can* be done. I guess it's like saying you could get your arm cut off without painkillers but *why would you.*

So these are some choices:

one hundred percent faithful for eighty-whatever years—*yeah, right*

cheat—*no thanks*

slut around, no commitment ever—*ewww, no*

abstinence—*not bloody likely*

Or… there's someone you love so very much. You devote your lives together. You have children you want to raise in a healthy, loving safe home. And together you have some fun. It's not for everyone, but it might be for us…

8

I LOOKED AT MATT'S TEXT again. I couldn't wait for him to get home. With Charlie off at his buddy's and Heather off at Jenna's for the night, I might even be able to convince Matt *and* get it started tonight. I glanced at the clock. *Ooooh* it was like waiting for water to boil. Come on already!

I decided to text Emma and see what she was up to tonight, just in case Matt was up for this. Actually, even if he wasn't, his text revealed he was up for some fun, so I was pretty sure he was up for some playtime at the very least!

I sent, *Hey, pretty girl! It's Leola from the other night. What's on the agenda tonight for you guys?* I decided to go to my room and pick out something sexy for tonight while I waited.

I opened my closet and my heart sank. Sparkly tank top (*boring*) mini skirt in blue, four black and red, two (*boring*) see-through dresses coming out my ass (*boring*), strappy, strapless, long-sleeved tops (*boring, boring, boring*)! I looked at the clock on my nightstand. Three thirty. I had two full hours before Matt got home. I went downstairs, grabbed my purse, and went to the garage.

Bling! *Hey, hon! So nice to hear from you! We have no plans tonight. I have to work till six and Steve's done at 5:30. I will talk to him and see if he's up for anything. I'll let you know ASAP.* Sweet!

Okay, hon. The kids' r gone for the night. I'll talk to Matt too.

Talk to Steve. We had a good time meeting you guys last weekend. Let's get together? I started the car and drove off, inhaling a deep, satisfied breath. Here's to hoping Matt was receptive to my plan. This was going to be incredibly *bad* fun.

I beat rush hour, getting home from the mall in record time. Dropping my bags on the bed, I grabbed my cell and texted Matt. *Hey, babe, can't wait for you to get home! Want to hang with S & E tonight?*

Knowing he would, I took the tags off my new garments and hopped in the shower. This was going to take some serious preparation. Fully shaved, buffed, and shined, I started to get ready for the *debauchery* night. My body vibrated with anticipation, like a waterfall rushing through my veins.

Bling! *Absolutely! See you shortly, xoxo*

I closed my phone. My blood felt like it was trying to burst out of my body. My fingers tingled. This was my poison. This was what made life worth living. This feeling right here. It was like a high, like a drug injected right into my veins. I only need a fix every once in a while, but when I needed it—*wow*—it blew me away every time.

When Matt got home it was all I could do not to bombard him before he got his coat off. It felt like he was purposely taking his time getting settled. *Don't you see me? Huh? Huh! Do ya? I know you can see me! Pay attention!* Like a bullet let off inside a steel room. *Boing-boing–boing…*

It was evident he could sense I needed to get this off my chest. He looked at me with a crooked smile. "What's up, babe?" *He knows me better than I know myself,* I think.

I laughed. "*Babe?* Whatever do you mean?" I playfully punched him. "I can't believe you made me wait so long to tell you! You're such a jerk! Are you *sure* you're ready to hear this? I have the most amazing idea…"

He gave me the reaction I was hoping for. He grabbed me around the waist and pulled me in close. "I can't wait to hear it, my love. You always have the best ideas." He gently pulled my hair and bit my neck. "Tell me."

9

BRINGING HIM OVER TO the bed, I patted the spot beside me for him to sit. He did one better and pulled me up to the pillows and we lay facing each other. We looked into each other's eyes, drinking each other in. Lucky didn't even begin to describe how I felt being his wife. I was so grateful for him. I kissed him.

"I know this is going to sound crazy, so I'd like you to listen with an open mind and don't interrupt until I'm done, okay? I've been trying to think of how to present this to you, but I can't come up with anything fancy, so I'm just going to say it."

I paused. He held my hand in his. I took a deep breath. "I don't know how I came up with this. It just came to me out of the blue. And if you're not up for it, I'll understand completely because it's way out there." I lowered my eyes so he could absorb this. "I was thinking we could get together with a couple, separately … but together. By separately I mean this. I have an 'affair'"—I air-quoted with my fingers—"with the guy and you have an affair with the woman. We know about it, we talk about it, we do everything 'together'"—again with the air quotes—"but as far as they're concerned, they're cheating on their spouse. They don't know the other is cheating, but we do. And we plan things and tell each other and still enjoy this together, but they don't know anything about anything except what we want them to know."

I didn't look up for what felt like forever. The silence in the room felt as if a heavy weight had been placed on us.

Matt didn't move; he lay there quietly. I slowly looked up and met his eyes. He looked at me funny. It was a look of intrigue, of curiosity, of *hmmmmmm…*

"I'm afraid to speak now!" I nervously laughed. "Please say something." I leaned in to kiss him, to make sure he didn't hate me for coming up with something so ludicrous.

"You." He smirked once I pulled away. He paused. "You are one fucked up chick."

I leaned back. I took in his full reaction, his posture, his vibe, whatever I could read.

"So fucked up, in fact, that I think you need help." He smiled as he said this to me.

I was confused. Did he like the idea? Was he planning our divorce and every other weekend with the kids?

"I want to know what you're saying!" I lay beside him, afraid to touch him, not sure if he was in or out. "Please don't torment me, you sadist!" I laughed. "Tell me what you honestly think. Please."

He took a deep breath and looked down. My eyes were glued to him. "I think that sounds like the most insane thing I've ever heard." He stopped. "And I'm game."

I let go of the breath I didn't realize I was holding. "Really? You don't hate me?"

"Not even possible, babe. I think we could have serious fun with this. But have you thought this through? Have you actually thought about me with another woman? Without you there? People who have affairs fall in love with people. *You* could fall in love with someone. I think in theory this would be super fuckin' fun, for sure! But think about it, *really* think about it. Me with another woman. You not there. Things could—"

"I trust you more than the world, babe," I interrupted. "I think you can do this more than anyone else could do it, and I think I could too. I think that as long as we're 100 percent honest with each other, we can even set up a video camera if you'd like, we could have some fun with it. People have affairs all the time. It would be like we're cutting off the deceit at the pass." *What an unexpected thought—wow.* "And if it doesn't work, at least *we're* in control and we can move on, maybe even never go down the *real* affair road with each other, possibly save our marriage from something that could potentially destroy us because we'll be driving this train."

Matt sat for a moment, pondering what I'd said. "You have a point, babe. You do." We laced our fingers as we sat with our thoughts. "You know we're gonna have to have some major rules laid out for this one, right? I mean, this isn't just some playful fun with each other. This is something totally different than swinging, right?" He almost read my thoughts.

"Oh for sure. Swinging was fun, but I feel like I just don't feel a big spark with it. It feels like a lot of work sometimes." Swinging *was* a lot of fun and still is sometimes, but I get restless. Shit, I worry sometimes what it will take for me to be "satisfied" with things. "And we'll have lots of rules, and I mean it when I say we can set up a video camera, a hidden one of course so we don't feel like anything is happening without us knowing; so there are no feelings of anyone ever lying, keeping things from the other or anything like that." *This* is *still for both of us. Just a little bit naughtier! I'm going to hell,* I laughed inside. "I texted Steve and Emma to see if they'd be up for hanging out tonight. I kind of came up with the idea when I thought of them, thought of hanging out. And I just thought, *Oh is this going to be just like a swinging thing again,* and I thought I'd like something more, something different, and that's when I came up with this. They seem like cool people who we're *both* attracted to." *Nothing like taking one for the team,* I thought cruelly. "And if you were up for something a little crazy, perhaps Steve and Emma could be who we do it with. What do you think?"

"Yeah, I think I could handle that," Matt said honestly. "They're both really cool, good looking, and I can definitely get turned on thinking of you with him," and he pulled me close, wrapped his arms around me, and kissed me hard.

My legs responded by wrapping around him, and we almost tore our clothes off each other in a frenzy of lust and need. Matt's arm went around me; he threw me on my back and rammed into me without notice. I cried out in surprise and raked my nails down his back. Pumping with mad fury, Matt grabbed my hair from the back of my head, and I clung to him, my legs high in the air. Within minutes it was over. We cried out together, and Matt collapsed on me, kissing me over and over again. *Fuck me, I love this man.*

Once our hearts calmed down we peeled our sweaty bodies off each other. With one more kiss Matt got up and went to the shower. I tried using the Jedi force to drag myself off the bed but reluctantly walked to the kitchen to retrieve my cell phone to see if Emma had written me back.

One new message. *Sweet! Hey, Leola, Steve is up for getting together tonight. The club?*

I walked back to our bedroom and yelled at Matt in the shower. "They're up for hanging out tonight. They suggested the club, what do you think?"

He made me wait while he finished. *Guys suck,* I thought. As *if* I can have a full shower in five minutes.

"Hmmmmm," he murmured. "Well, yeah, let's go to the club, get the vibe going for sure." Matt was thinking out loud. "It's Friday night, it'll be busy. If we're going to do this, we need to do it now. It needs to be established before we set a 'swingers' relationship with them, right? I think the first night with you and Emma is as far as we should go that way with them. We should definitely get on this path as soon as possible."

"I agree. If it's busy enough, you can keep her occupied and I'll keep him occupied, and we'll plant some seeds. But it needs to be subtle, you know?" I stopped. We were both quiet, thinking. We looked at each other, held eyes for a moment, and then burst into laughter.

I wonder if we'll be allowed to be together in hell.

10

THERE ARE ALL KINDS of affairs:
- Emotional
- Sexual
- "I fell out of love"
- "I'm just a whore"
- "I'm going to get back at you"
- "I need to feel desirable again"
- "I'm bored"
- "I want out of this relationship so I'm going to cheat so my partner will finally leave me because I don't have the balls to just be honest and use my grown up words and do it myself."
- This one's my favorite: "Oh, I got drunk and it was an 'accident'—'cause you know how your penis *accidentally* fell into her pussy or how your vagina *accidentally* fell onto his cock.
- "It's not really an affair, she or he was gonna leave his or her spouse, so we're not really cheating, we're in love."
- The seven-year-itch
- "You're gonna use sex to control our relationship? Well watch this!"
- "I just need the thrill again."

The list is endless. Ask anyone why they had an affair and it's going to be a different reason every time. But really, they're under one category or another. That's really not important, is it?

They are all about lying and deceit, and if they're found out, they're one of the most damaging things anyone can go through, because the cheated *on* is the only one who serves the life sentence.

And don't try to tell yourself anything else. It *is* a life sentence. No matter what forgiving, counseling, understanding, or "we worked it out" bullshit you went through, the one you cheated on will serve this sentence till the day he or she dies. Forever worried, forever watching, always wondering.

Unless the death is a result of the affair. Or the cheater dies…

So *why… how…* could I come up with something so cruel as to purposely set someone up to go through this? I hear you! It sounds so awful, I couldn't agree more. I think it's more of a self-preservation for me. You have to understand, *please* understand, how much I love my husband. He is so very amazing. He is an incredible lover—I seriously can't reiterate this enough. He is *fuck me sideways* amazing in bed, between the making love and after we go to the club, it is so great, it is the perfect mix of the good, the bad, and the ugly. He is my *best* friend and is the father of my children. He makes me feel special, loved, and cherished. Nothing is more important to me than keeping our relationship strong and beautiful; not only for us but for our children.

I feel like this: right or wrong, the people who are going to cheat on their spouses are going to cheat on their spouses, regardless of Matt and me getting involved. Some people cheat, some people don't *cough* *bullshit*. Anyone we approach is either going to turn us down or be all for it. The "all for it" people are going to do it with us or with someone else. I am preserving *my* relationship. Not theirs.

Matt and I met when we were both taking classes to become realtors. Matt is a commercial realtor, and I am a residential realtor. We both have a mutual respect for each other, and we own our own realty company, a small one in LA called Open House.

And now ... we have an open marriage. Well, sort of open. Ahhh, the circle of life. Makes me smile in a rub-your-hands-together-and–laugh-evilly (like Mr. Burns on *The Simpsons*) kind of way.

In fifteen years of marriage, we have kept busy enough to not get bored with each other. We also make trips every year with our kids. The last trip was a Disney cruise. The kids had a blast; even too-cool Charlie had so much fun. Family trips are the best, aren't they? They help us reconnect with each other. Remind ourselves we are on the same team, fighting for the same things, working toward the same goals. Working at having a family that is a functioning part of society is important, and raising kids with values is important to us. We're just like you. We all want the same things for our kids and our relationships. How we go about them is perhaps different, but we all just try. We don't have all the answers (*well I do; just ask*), but we are all just trying to do the best with what we have, with what we know. We all have our broken childhoods, our embarrassing stories, our memories we can't let go of. And life moves forward and we move on and we try. We try and we fail. And we try some more.

As far as I know Matt has never cheated on me. I cheated on him once, but he doesn't know about it. It was with a girl, and it happened post-wedding, pre-children. I was out for a friend's bachelorette party, and we were bar hopping, dancing, drinking ... we had a fun, fun night! I think there were eight or nine of us and I knew most of them except a few who were friends of Christie's from her childhood.

Her name was Lori, and she was so sexual—you know what I mean? She exuded sexuality. Her hair was funky—all different colors—and she wore too much eye makeup and weird clothes and had piercings and tattoos. When we finished with the bar hopping, we headed back to Christie's house, and that's where it happened. I didn't mean for anything to happen (my favorite "I was drunk" affair, remember?). There was so much sexual tension between us it felt natural for it to go that way. Hot drunk girls, shooters, and scantily dressed, boobies bouncing all over the place ... the night is bound to flow that way. What's a girl to do?

With the music up way too loud, we were in the kitchen and Lori turned to me and pressed a shooter between my pushed up breasts—*thank you Victoria's Secret*—leaned over, and buried her face in my cleavage. I held the back of her head, laughing, and as her head came up, my hands fell to her hips. She finished her shooter and licked her lips. I pulled her to me and kissed her. I didn't think twice about it. She wrapped her arms around my waist and kissed me back. She tasted like Sambuca and her lips were full and her tongue was firm.

When I pulled away, we locked eyes and walked down the hall, still holding together kissing until we found Christie's bedroom. We fell on the bed and made out forever. I pulled her tank top off and she was braless, exposing her full breasts, and I lowered my mouth on to them and sucked, flicking her nipple between my parted lips. She held my head, twisting her fingers in my hair, and I came up and kissed her again. I removed her panties from under her skirt. I gently slipped my fingers into her warm, wet hole as I kissed her hard. She moaned into my mouth. I was soaking wet. This was so new for me. It felt awkward but natural at the same time. I tentatively put my fingers into my pussy and brought up some for her to taste. She sucked on my fingers, and I kissed her so I could taste it too. Fuck me, I tasted good in her mouth.

She was so soft, I explored her forever. She touched and tasted me, and when we were both sated, we lay there together for a long time, hands roaming, the softness so foreign to us both, both of us our first time with a woman forever etched in memory. I couldn't get enough. I held her breasts like they were precious and breakable, touching, softly rubbing every crevice of her. We fell asleep like that in each other's arms.

I fell in love with Lori that night. I fell in love with the closeness we had, with the bond. I fell in love with the softness and the appreciation you can have for women. She personified the intangible beauty that encompasses a woman for what we are. Perhaps I fell in love with myself a bit, looking back. With the acknowledgement that I am beautiful, with the acceptance of what I have to offer as damaged as I am, as we all are just trying to get through this life unscathed. That through it all we will be okay and we're all worth it.

I woke up shortly after and left her there sleeping. We never saw each other again. There were no cell phones back then, so we lost touch. Life happens, and we move on.

11

I HOPPED IN THE SHOWER (*again, had some freshening up to do thanks to Matt*), did a quick wash, and then proceeded to do my hair and makeup and get dressed in my new clothes.

Matt got out of the shower, dressed, brushed his teeth in forty-five seconds flat, and went to watch TV. The general frustration about men getting ready aside, I just love getting all dolled up to go out, don't you? I *love* it. It's so fun. Even though I'm in my mid-(*ahem* *late*)-thirties, I still feel like I'm in my twenties—*and yes, I still look it, dammit*. No matter the age, getting all dolled up will never get old.

I turned on the stereo and closed the door so Matt would be spared my *amazing* singing voice while I sexied up.

Remembering Emma's text, I grabbed my cell. *Hey, darlin! We'll meet you at the club tonight. See you soon. xo.*

Standing in the bathroom, I watched myself in the mirror putting curls in my hair and thought about Steve and Emma. I hoped this would be as fun and exciting as I was anticipating.

Emma was fun. She had a beautiful smile and pretty, wide-set eyes with nondescript hair, kind of a medium-brown, medium length. I'd say she was about five feet, eight inches with an attractive body—a little soft, but with that came a nice rack and a kickin' booty, as I deliciously remembered.

Steve was not much taller than me—with my heels on, that is.

He had messy, dark hair that made his eyelashes dark, so when he looked at you, you had to look through the natural eyeliner appearance to discover their chocolate color. His hands were big, strong. Since I didn't play with him at all last weekend, I didn't know if there were any tattoos on him. Of course I couldn't wait to find out.

All hot and sexied-up, I went to meet Matt, who was waiting for me in the living room still watching TV. I have never been one of those girls who took three hours to get ready. Thirty minutes from shower to heels walking out the door for the most part was my average, so Matt never got frustrated waiting for me. He whistled when I walked in—*good boy*—and got up off the couch. I chose black Capri leggings tonight with a cherry-red, rayon, over-the-shoulder flowing shirt that came down just above my ass, and black heels. Completing the look with all the right jewelry and some perfume, I was ready to knock Steve's socks off—now that I'd revved up my husband, of course.

When Steve and Emma entered the club, I was so excited. Emma looked beautiful with a loose, silky dress that cut down so far it looked like it would have to be taped to her breasts so they wouldn't fall out. She wore little black strappy heels, and her hair was done up here and there so it looked all messy; her curls were spiked up in all directions.

My heart did a disappointed little flip as I realized she could never be mine again, but I put that away quickly as I realized Steve would be all mine, alone. He complemented her look with a casual T-shirt and jeans, a look that let Emma shine without looking too dressed up.

Matt squeezed my hand as we sat at the table waiting for them to make their drinks. We got up when they came over and gave them each a hug and a kiss and picked up where we had left off last weekend. Except this time, I made sure to hold Steve's gaze when I was sure Emma wasn't watching—and as I'd suspected, I felt Steve responding to me. So much so that I made sure I touched him under the table with my calf and foot when I could—small touches at first, quickly brushing against him.

Then I started leaving my leg on his longer and longer. I watched Matt with Emma. I couldn't tell what he was doing differently, if anything. We all talked as a group of four for a long while. Then at one point, after leaving my leg on Steve's for a moment too long, I brushed it against him as a good-bye and asked Emma to dance. If I couldn't have her in this game we'd invented, I was not going to let any opportunity slip by to enjoy what I could. And that included, at the very least, I decided then, kissing her. In the lifestyle, that's almost expected. Without at least that, Steve and Emma might get suspicious, I rationalized.

When we got back to the table Matt got up to get me a drink and Emma went to the little girls' room. That left Steve and me alone for a precious few minutes. I had to use my time wisely without overdoing it.

"Emma's amazing," I said. "How long have you guys been together?"

"Thanks. I like her too." He smiled at me, acting all casual. "We've been together for about four years now, married for almost four of them too," he added. I raised my eyebrows. "I just knew she was the one," he finished.

I smiled. I looked at Steve. Man, this was going to be hard …. Such deliberate flirting was *not* my forte. In my peripheral vision, I noticed Matt coming back to the table with my drink. "Do you want to dance with me, Steve?" was all I could think of.

"Yes I do," he said, and I winked at my husband as I took my drink from him and took a long swallow, set it down, and met Steve on the dance floor. Now I could keep his attention while Matt could be alone with Emma.

It was a slow song, which is why I suggested it. I made sure my center was pressed into him a little tighter than before. His mouth was near my ear, and I turned my head until his lips touched me. It was dark in the club, as usual. The lighting darkened a bit more to create a sort of private ambiance when slow songs came on. He pulled me close and put his head down slightly so he was in the crook of my neck. I felt him subtly inhale my scent. I pulled my hair over so he could kiss my neck if he wanted, and we danced silently like that for most of the song. I tried to keep one eye on Matt without being obvious. *Such hard work.* Before the song ended, I whispered to Steve, "Can I have your cell number?" He looked at me then. I tilted my head slightly and smiled, a tiny secret smile only he could see.

And he kissed me. Then he pulled me close and whispered, "I'll give it to Matt, and you can get it off his phone so no one gets suspicious."

And that is how it's done.

Now I was hoping Matt did his part. As we came back to the table I leaned into my husband and kissed his cheek, lingering there long enough to make a reconnection with him. His arm went around my back, and he pulled me between his legs as he sat on the stool. I gave him another playful kiss, smiling at him and then to Steve and Emma. Matt was all smiles, and behind my back, as I was facing the table, he squeezed my hand in his long enough for me to know the deal was sealed. I grabbed my drink, took a healthy swallow, and pulled my husband on to the dance floor. A country whirl to "Friends in Low Places" was the perfect way to complete our secret circle.

When the song ended, Matt leaned over and said in my ear, "Let's get out of here." I grabbed my purse and checked my cell phone. I leaned over to Emma, and over the dance music I yelled that our youngest is at a sleepover but is not feeling well, that I just got a text to please come get her, so we were going to have to head out. Of course this was a lie, but we needed to end this night with them where we were. We didn't want to go the swinger's route with them anymore.

She pouted and nodded, and we all gave big hugs and kisses to each other. We lingered with the other's spouses a moment extra this time and left the club floating on a cloud of excitement. My insides were on fire; I felt the heat racing through my body. I was a volcano quivering to erupt at any moment. I couldn't wait to get this show on the road! I couldn't *wait* to tell Ever. I wished she was here to see the whole thing. She'd be high-fiving and fist-pumping me the whole way.

During the drive home, I turned on the stereo and took off my seatbelt. Matt leaned back while I unzipped his jeans, and he popped out, ready for me. I took him in my mouth and he gasped, trying to stay on the road.

"Easy, babe," he warned.

I slowed my rhythm.

"That's not better!" He laughed.

I smiled but didn't stop. The twenty-minute drive home felt too short, but I was thankful. I didn't want him to cum. I was soaking wet by the time we pulled into the driveway. We furiously scrambled into the house as I started to undress Matt at the front door. Once he finally got me inside, he dropped the keys, shut the door, and grabbed me in the foyer.

His hands burrowed into my hair as he grabbed my head and kissed me while I pulled his jeans down over his hips and wrapped my hand around his member. He pushed me onto my knees, and I took him in my mouth again. Matt held on to the wall and moaned. I felt him getting too hard, a telltale sign he was about to cum. I stood up and walked away from him to give him a moment to calm down. I slowly peeled off my clothes for him to watch as I walked down the hall to our bedroom. He locked the front door and followed me down.

I just made it to the bed when he grabbed me from behind. He pushed my head down and thrust inside me. I cried out, begging for it harder. Grabbing my hips from behind he pumped harder and harder and I banged against him, rising up for the deepest fit. He fucked me hard, my face in the sheets as I clung to the bed. He was buried deep. I felt him hitting me inside and begged for more. He thrust deeper, if that's possible, grunting with the exertion. I cried out in ecstasy, not wanting him to stop, but I didn't want him to cum so I pushed him back and turned around and kissed him hard.

I turned him around and wet my fingers from my soaking wet, throbbing pussy and gently stuck them in Matt's perfect ass. He sucked in his breath and I stopped, but he quietly begged for more. He bent over the bed and I wet my fingers again. I leaned over, and with my other hand I stroked his cock. He cried out as I fucked him as he'd just fucked me. I bit his back and clung to him as I wet my fingers again. I was so wet my juices dripped down my thighs. I needed to cum, it felt like I was burning on fire. I stood up and turned him over and rode him so fucking hard. His cock rubbed furiously deep inside me. We came together, screaming in unison, grabbing sheets, hips, and shoulders till we fell together. Silent.

12

I THINK IT'S QUITE UNFAIR that we are forced (in an unspoken manner) to choose one sex to be attracted to. Our society is slowly opening up to "other" possibilities, but it is taking too long, quite frankly. It seems daft that even liberal cultures pressure us into attraction to one gender or the other. What exactly is the genius rationale for having to choose? Really, since the advent of hand washing and antibiotics, the human population is doing quite fucking fine, thank you very much. And I could have sworn it's been at least a *few* weeks since the dawn of birth control pills, condoms, and STD testing. Maybe I missed a memo somewhere?

So, if not for the necessity of procreation, why do we still insist sex can't occasionally be for simple, wet, messy, naughty, sweet pleasure? Personally, I appreciate both genders and find equally physically stimulating. I mean, have you seen the V lines on a man's abs poking accidentally out of his shirt? Have you seen a woman's thigh quiver when she orgasms? Come on! I dare you to put your indoctrinated moral blueprints aside and tell me that biologically it doesn't make your damn gonads twitch! I would bet that most men at a Bon Jovi concert back in the '80s or Nirvana jam in the '90s—depending on your genre of music— had wood (*don't fucking deny it*). And there isn't a woman on the planet who didn't have a girlfriend in high school whose soft gaze, soft hair, and soft lips didn't make her wet.

So why is it that he can like shitty flavorless beer *and* whiskey or she can like riding her hippy bike with the flower on the basket *and* driving her SUV. That seems blindingly hypocritical to me. And yet, the moral snobbery of predetermined, useless stigma on "penis and vagina for procreation only" dictates we are only to appreciate pleasure from the opposite gender. Or, as we are *finally* starting to accept, the same gender—but not both? I say these ancient made-up judgments need a good blindfolded rim job or a soft face between your thighs, and then come talk to me!

And really… at the end of the day, it's about loving and appreciating life. That should go for whomever you chose to make love to. Consensually, of course. I guess we're called bisexuals. And we are stigmatized by the straight and gay community alike. There's something catastrophically ironic about being sexually judged by a twenty-year-old lesbian who just came out of the closet, or even the forty-year-old gay man who's had to keep it a secret for so many years, living a lie for fear of being ostracized by family, friends, and society. The look on their faces as they try to explain their judgment in "rational" terms without using the same destructive, bigoted bullshit lingo that was dished out to them all those years is shockingly sincere. I'm sure the expression on my face would look similar to the one they gave every time someone knocked down their community.

But as everyone is fighting for a voice, perhaps one day bisexual people will have our day to hold our heads up high. I guess more than anything we just really don't give a shit to fight for it. We are a camouflaged group. We are a dirty little secret. We are judged as transient, indecisive sluts. But we do have the lovely option of changing our sexual colors in public spaces where we feel at risk. We are amorous chameleons because it's just plain asinine to fight for something that should never have been an issue in the first place. But hey, that's just my opinion. It's not like one bisexual heathen's opinion is going to make a big difference in the grand scheme of things anyway. Besides, I'm no politician, and taboo is just plain fun!

So thanks to all the straight-laced homosexuals and straight-laced heterosexuals who make my sex life twice as fun! I'll be happy to make mad, consensual, taboo, safe, filthy love to your partner in all the ways you were too scared to try when your inflexible pious bigotry gets old.

13

SATURDAY MORNINGS ARE ALWAYS my favorite. It feels like it's always nice out, always ready to be the best day of the week, like it's constantly trying to prove its worth. Pulling the covers away, with a playful tug I woke Matt. He full-body stretched and pushed my head down and almost made me gag. He laughed as I squirmed, trying to get free.

"*Hey!*" I squealed as I gasped and pulled away. "Is that any way to thank me?" I hit him in the leg.

He caved and pulled me up to him for a snuggle and kissed my head. "Soooo... *that* was some fun last night. Too drunk and horny to ask how yours played out. Do tell." Matt pushed himself up on one elbow.

I told him about playing with Steve with my leg.

"Nice. Very nice..." He approved.

And then I told him about the dancing. "I was surprised at how easy it was. I don't think they really have any idea what the swinger's lifestyle is about, truly. I don't know any swinger who would jump over to cheating, especially so soon into experimenting, but hey, who am I to judge?"

Matt agreed.

"What did you do? I was so busy with what I was doing and keeping Steve from getting suspicious about you two I didn't notice anything."

Matt lifted his shoulders and smiled with his full teeth, which translates to *I am twelve years old and got my first hand-job* excitement. I couldn't help but laugh.

"Well, it was pretty hard with you sitting right there, to be honest. So when you and Steve got up to dance, I just asked her."

My eyebrow shot up.

"Yeah, it was pretty easy. I just said to her, 'Is it okay if I ask you something private? Just between us, and if I am crossing any lines, please just tell me.' At that point, she took my hand and said of course. So I leaned over the table and said 'Would you ever consider hanging out, just the two of us?' And she hesitated and looked at Steve."

I was on the edge of my seat waiting for her answer.

"And then she looked back at me and said, 'I would.' And I told her the song was almost over, let's act natural, and I would get her cell number from your phone. Then we talked about what we were doing for the weekend, and by that time the song was over and you and Steve came back to the table. That was it. How'd I do?"

I was impressed. He did very well. "Wow, babe." I shrugged and gave a big smile. "Let's give it a couple days to sink in and … yeah." I didn't know what to say. This was really going to happen…. It's a crazy feeling inside. So exciting. So wrong. Like getting on a roller coaster. *Here we go!*

Matt leaned in for a kiss. "I love you so much."

I kissed him right back and clung tightly to him. And then we made sweet love. I mean *sweet* love, *madly-in-love* love. Drink-me-in, drown-in-my-eyes, make-you-cry love. The whole world fell away. It was only us. Nothing else mattered.

After showers and a light snack, Matt went to pick up Heather and I tidied up. I wanted to pick her up so I could see Sam again, but I thought, *Let's not push it.* Clothes were strewn all over the house—nice image for your children to come home to, right? Yeah, I didn't think so either.

When Charlie got home we went about our weekend with vigor, complete with chores, laughter, friends, and family. It was all I could do to keep focused on the here and now. I was excited to get a few texts over to Steve and Emma to see where this was headed. If Matt felt any anxiety over it he didn't show it at all, which frustrated me. How could he not be thinking of this? I felt like I was on one of those vibrating machines designed to help with circulation. I could almost feel my teeth chattering from it. But Matt was all calm cool and collected. *Asshole.*

On Sunday I called Ever to meet for a walk. I felt like I was going to explode and had to tell her everything. We'd hung out the night before, but too many people were there, too many ears that could hear. I'm a mom—I *know* how much I can hear when my friends are talking amongst themselves.

First thing she did was give me shit that I hadn't called sooner. I apologized eagerly and told her to shut up and listen. We walked quickly, the same pace as I talked, the words flowing out like a broken fire hydrant, spewing water out all over the streets in every direction. Only there will be no playing children in this metaphor.

Ever gave all the right noises and comments and let me talk. When I was finished, all she could say was, "Holy shit!"

I couldn't agree more. We found a bench to sit on under the trees, the leaves almost fully filled in, granting us some much-needed shade for our sweaty bodies.

"Okay, so listen," she started, "Are you guys *sure* you want to do this? I mean, it's pretty scary. What if Matt falls in love with her? From what you've told me, she sounds pretty amazing."

"I know. And yes I've thought about it. I *have*," I emphasized when I saw Ever's doubtful look. "I just think if your spouse is going to cheat, he's going to cheat, there's nothing much you can do about it. You can't lock him in the house forever. This way, maybe we can have some power over how it happens." I tried to convince her. She had her doubts and I could respect that. Hell, I had my *own* fears, but I felt like this was so planned out, there wasn't much for error.

"There's *always* room for error, Lee. They're *men*, for Christ's sake!"

We laughed.

"I know. But," I said, gaining some confidence, "I trust my husband. *You* know Matt. He's one of the good ones. This is going to be fun!"

"Okay," she said doubtfully. "There's just no such thing as sanctity of marriage anymore, is there? That's why I stay with Clint." She laughed. "*No* chick is going to fuck that ugly fucker!" She shrieked.

I laughed so hard tears streamed down my face. A truer statement has never been declared.

Monday night after dinner we decided to go down to the park for a walk. It is an Indian Reserve Park just a few minutes' drive from our house. There are so many trails, parks, fields, and creeks running through it, so beautiful. We like to come down from time to time to stay connected with nature, get out of the concrete jungle, and breathe in some fresh air.

After my walk with Ever, I'd realized we hadn't gone walking as a family since the autumn before. Heather loved looking for different leaves, cool rocks, and things like that. Charlie liked stealing the rocks from Heather and throwing them as far as he could. Matt and I always walked hand in hand behind them, laughing at their antics. Sometimes we talk and talk, sometimes we are so quiet, just drinking everything in and appreciating it all.

Today we talked. It's rare to get time to talk when the kids are this age. Well, I guess it's 50/50. They can be gone for hours at a time, with friends or watching a movie or something, and other times they just want to be with us all the time. So we used the time we had on this day to plan our next move.

"I'd like you to text Emma soon—maybe tonight," I suggested to Matt. "We shouldn't let too much time go by, you know?" He nodded and agreed. "I think I'll text Steve tomorrow during the day. Actually, I guess we should both do it during the day. We both know their partner is home at night, so that would be dumb to do it tonight."

"For sure," Matt agreed. "What should we say? It has to be inconspicuous. Something neutral, like, 'Hey there, what're you doing' kind of thing." He paused.

"Exactly. And when they write back something like, 'I'm working,' just go with it from there. I don't want to plan those things out unless we're stuck. It won't sound natural. But it's important we save all the texts to stay with the honesty deal."

"Of course, babe." Matt squeezed my hand. "We have to keep that in the forefront of our minds all the time."

"Okay, let's do it tomorrow. That makes it four days since we started this, which is more than enough time. We need to keep this from dragging out too much. I want it to be fast and hard and fun and bad and ..." I laughed as Matt grabbed me around the head and tried to pull me down. "You're going have to do better than that, Mr. Matt Man!" I struggled free and ran from him, chasing the kids as he chased me. We ran like that all the way back to the car.

When we got home we had a snack and put the kids to bed. We poured ourselves a couple of drinks and snuggled up on the couch to watch a movie. With Matt's strong arms around me, I forgot all about our little scheme for a while and molded to his body and thoroughly enjoyed our flick.

14

THE NEXT MORNING AFTER I dropped the kids off at their respective schools, I drove to work. It wasn't a long drive, only about twenty minutes, and I channel surfed the whole way, stopping on fantastic songs and belting out every word to those favorites. I didn't even care who saw me. I am a fantastic singer. No seriously, I am. In the car. By myself. It's incredible, really. If you heard me, you would be shocked—I sound like exactly the singer I'm singing along with.

I wonder if sarcasm translates to paper as well as it sounds in my head as I'm writing this?

When I got to work, Cassie was already there, on the phone as usual. She was so busy these days. Cassie sold mostly condos, and they were really selling well lately. Coming out of an economic depression, people were scraping enough money together for condos for home ownership. We all have to start somewhere. I mostly sold houses, big ones if I could help it, but I'd take any house at this point. I don't like to handle condos but will for a friend; otherwise; I send it over to Cassie. Doesn't matter much either way; I get a cut of her sales as she is my employee.

I walked past her and placed her coffee on her desk and went to my office. She blew me a kiss of thanks. My small office faced the front of my store. Matt has the desk opposite Cassie's in the open area. He's not here very often. He takes care of the properties we own for our renters, so he's out a lot taking care of renovations, lawn, repairs, and such in addition to selling his commercial listings. He mostly works out of his truck when he can. He hates being stuck in the office.

This morning I was dying for it to be late enough to text Steve. I didn't want to text him too early as he might be busy and that would make me have to wait that much longer for him to write back, which would just make me nuts. So I busied myself returning calls, answering e-mails, and paperwork. When my computer showed 9:23, I thought *fuck it* and grabbed my cell.

Hey there... it's Leola—busy? I hit send. Immediately goose bumps stood up on my arms. *So exciting!* I put my phone down and checked my Facebook page. I looked at my computer again. It was 9:24. *For fuck's sake, are you kidding me?*

I sat there, frustrated.

Bling! Finally! I grabbed my phone. He wrote, *Hi! I'm just at work. Took you long enough! :P*

I smiled. *Shit. now I have to come up with a clever Facebook status aaand something witty to say to Steve.* Argh!

I sighed and scrunched my lips. I texted, *LOL I know, sorry. Busy weekend with the family. Thought about you lots though. Does that count?* I sent it and set down my phone.

Bling! *It sure does. I did too. Thought about a lot of things...*

Wow. This was going to be easier than I thought. I put the phone down and thought, *What can I say I don't want to be too forward; that's no fun.* Guys like to take the lead with stuff like this. So I have to play along so he doesn't feel overpowered, but I still have to be in control of this.

I typed, Really... with me?

Play it coy—we're pretending here, right? Might as well play all the way then. Then my cell rang and I went into work mode for a few hours. Steve wrote me back, but I left his text unread while I took care of business. Guys like a little hard to get, don't they?

A few hours later, when I finally had a minute, I checked

my texts. There were a couple from Matt, telling me he'd made contact, I texted him back that I had too.

Steve's text was waiting for me to read when I had a few minutes. He wrote, *Fuck yeah with you. You make me so hard.*

Yeah I do, I laughed.

I wrote back, *Would there be any way I could help you with that?*

His text back was almost immediate. He must've been on pins and needles the whole morning. *Sooner than later, please.*

Well, I thought, *I'll just have to check with my husband on what would be a good time for him.* I laughed so hard all by myself. I'm going to hell. I texted, *I'll let u know when.*

And I left it at that for today.

Sated for the time being, I drove home in relatively the same manner as I drove to work—in the same manner as every day: at the top of my lungs and unapologetically off key.

When Matt came home, we smiled into each other's eyes and went in for a big hug and kiss. Then we went about our business putting our shit away, turning on the TV to watch the news in the background, and getting things ready for supper. The kids were downstairs watching TV, having already done their homework. With a few minutes of free time on our hands, we swapped cells.

I went to Matt's messages, opened the thread from Emma, and scrolled on his iPhone to the top of the messages. The first one was from Matt, of course. Just saying, *Here's my cell number if you want it … Matt.*

Hey Matt… she wrote.

The majority of the texts were small-talk. Emma finally got down to business:

So, you still wanna hang out sometime?

I really would, Emma, he texted.

:) Me too.

Matt took the reins. Very nice. *Let me find out when I can get away and I'll let you know … can't wait to see you again.*

They made a date for Thursday afternoon.

I smiled. "Nice work, babe," I said, looking up. Matt was just finishing up reading mine.

"Wow, you too. Steve doesn't fuck around, does he?"

I could picture Ever as a fly on the way, frozen in disbelief watching us. Inside I was laughing, thinking of the hilarity at her expense, thoroughly enjoying the fact that I had one up on her, which didn't happen often.

"I know, right? I was thinking he'd send more subtle texts when he's sober, but he surprised me." I gave him back his cell. "So Thursday, huh? I think we can make some time Thursday. Should I do Thursday too? No I don't think I should. I should do tomorrow or Friday—what do you think?"

"Definitely. I think you should do tomorrow for sure, if you can. He'll still be riding a high into Thursday and won't care if Emma's in a *meeting*, right?"

"Okay," I said, surprised by Matt's enthusiasm. "How far are we going this first time? If you think about it, it could go any way. I can 'forget' to bring a condom, but Steve's a guy, so he'll probably remember. I could say I have my period, but Emma could bring a condom *and* not have her period. I don't know how much we can go at the same pace as each other."

"No, you're right," Matt said. "That's too hard and would feel staged. I think we're in this, right? We're in it for the whole nine yards, so we can't nitpick every detail. We can only control what we control. So we go into this guns ablazin' and go from there. Now I *do* have a very important question. How long are we going to keep this 'affair' going? And what is the frequency that we're going to meet?"

We turned at the sound of feet bounding up the stairs. "Hi, Mommy! Hi, Daddy!" Heather brightens up any room she enters. "Can I have a snack?"

I handed her a banana. "You can have this if you'd like, but we're going to have supper soon."

She grabbed it and went back downstairs, closing the door behind her.

I faced my husband. I puckered my lips, thinking. "Well,

what do you think? No more than once a week, and no more than a few months?"

Matt thought this through. "That sounds reasonable. One thing I do *not* want to do is to start, like, comparing how many times 'this is happening to you and it's not happening to me the same amount' kind of thing. Does that make sense? Like if you and Steve have sex every time you get together, and the last time Emma and I get together we didn't go all the way or something like that. I don't want to start tit for tatting. We're in it for what it's going to be, not to compete with each other."

"Deal. Now let's get some supper going before someone calls social services on us for starving our poor children."

15

THAT NIGHT I SLEPT like a baby—once I fell asleep, that is. I went over tomorrow's schedule in my head. If it didn't work out for Steve to get away, then we would plan for Friday or we could even do Thursday morning. Wow, that would be a busy day for us! I walked through my morning: getting up, showering, and texting what I would say to try to get him to meet. Finally, I forced myself to stop thinking and fell asleep. I had instructed Matt not to wake me in the morning. I love making my own hours. I wanted to be well rested for my fun-filled day ahead!

Just before I fell asleep, guilt about Emma crept in. It would've been nice to have been true friends with her. But I pushed those feelings away, telling myself she felt the same about me, knowing she was going to fuck my husband too.

I dressed that morning in nice work clothes with some pretty matching lingerie. The drive to work was uneventful—except for the live concert going on at eighty mph down the freeway, that is.

My iPhone tweeted at me, signaling a text. When I finally came to a stop at a light, I checked my phone. It was Matt. *Good luck, my sweet love. I love you. Enjoy your day!! xoxo*

When I got to work I wrote him back. *Jackass! LOL xoxo*

Finding Steve's thread, I texted him too. *Morning—busy this afternoon?*

I got my things together and tried to focus on getting through the morning if Steve accepted my indecent proposal.

Morning, beautiful. I can get away. Want me to make the arrangements?

I was blown away. Was this really how this all worked? Could people really go through life doing this so easily? All of a sudden it felt cheap. I felt myself shrinking back, like a balloon that a child has let the air out of. I felt let down almost, but I wasn't ready to give up. *Shit. Shit shit shit.*

I thought about talking to Matt about this. I thought it should be once every few weeks to a month of getting together, of planning things, of plans falling through. The anticipation needed to be heightened. It couldn't be this easy—that's when it gets boring.

So with that decision made I texted him back, keeping Matt and my plans to go through with this now but then keeping the tease going for the next few weeks to build it up further next time. I decided to play with him for a few texts at least. The tension needed to be built back up for today or I wasn't going to be happy.

What color shirt are you wearing today? I asked him.

Grey, he texted back.

Oh, shit… if you were wearing a green shirt, I would've been all for fucking your brains out this afternoon … too bad … I smiled. I'm so funny. That's how you play hard to get, Steve. Have *some* fun with it, man! Don't just flop down in front of me. That's not sexy, I secretly scolded him.

Sonofabitch. I'm not wearing a green shirt until two weeks from now! he teased.

Thank you! Now we're having fun! *For fuck's sake, man— and I'm gonna be SICK that day!! :(* I sent.

That's okay. I didn't want to fuck you anyway, he wrote back.

Nice one, Steve, I smiled. *Good, 'cause wherever we're meeting this afternoon better be in a public place so you don't touch me at all.*

Cassie brought me some soup and a roll for lunch and we ate together. She told me about her dating life, her online dating experiences, and her speed-dating nightmare, and we laughed and talked all through lunch. She was finally seeing someone, she told me, after all the horror she'd divulged. Her name was Karen and she was a hottie, a tattoo artist who worked downtown. My eyebrows went up. She had perfect big tits, Cassie explained, and a pussy that didn't quit. We laughed together.

I fucking loved Cassie. She was my kind of shit. She'd come to us right out of school. The sister of a friend of mine who we'd met at a mutual friend's birthday a few years ago. Matt and I weren't looking, but the three of us got to chatting and a friendship was born. Cassie was a go-getter, we could tell right off the bat. There was no loss for us if it didn't work out, so we thought we'd give it a try. What's perfect about it is she works the hours she wants to work. She pays us part of her commission, and other than that, she is her own boss.

I told her I would be out doing some shopping this afternoon as I had a few hours of slack time. She would be out this afternoon anyway, she said. She had a showing and then was going to hit the gym. Perfect.

When Steve told me where we were going to meet, I got nervous. I'd brought my toothbrush to work so I could freshen up. The hotel he had booked for us was only about seven blocks away from my shop, and since it was a nice enough outside I decided to walk to kill time and get there hopefully before he did. By the time I got there I had twenty minutes to spare. After picking up the room card key I went straight to the room number he'd texted to me.

It was a standard room. King-size bed, windows with heavy drapes, bathroom. A normal hotel room. I closed the drapes almost all the way and turned off the lights. It was still light, but the "ugly light" effect was gone and made a middle-of-the-day romp slightly more romantic. At the last minute I decided to go through my phone and pick out some music and put together a quick playlist. Putting it on shuffle, I pressed play and then paused it and waited for Steve.

16

IT IS AN INTERESTING feeling, sitting there waiting for someone other than your spouse to walk into the room to touch you, taste you, feel you in ways only reserved for your husband. I know we had done the swinging thing already, so being with another man other than my husband wasn't new to me. What *was* new was being with another man without my husband there to connect with. This time was for me. Not for us.

I wished I had a drink to take the edge off. *Should've had wine with lunch,* I thought. I walked around the room, taking in the pictures, the way the lamps were placed throughout the room, what the soaps smelled like in the bathroom. Coming early was definitely off my list of things to do next time. There is something to be said about being fashionably late.

I went back to the little table in the corner and picked up my phone again and checked my Facebook. Nothing much new there. No new texts either, so I sent a quick one to Ever: *Here goes nothing! Wish me luck!* and a text to Matt: *I love you, babe.*

Ever immediately texted me back, as I knew she would: *Yer a bitch—ride that cowboy!*

I gasped and laughed at the same time. She always knew the right things to say, even though she was full of shit. I knew she wasn't on board with this, but she smiles and supports you through anything. I think she does it so she can gleefully chant

I told you so! It's her favorite part. She's lucky I get her. It's a fun part of our friendship.

Shut up, you bitch, haha, I wrote back and put the phone on silent. Then I affixed my iPhone back to the iPod again. And I waited some more.

What if he changes his mind? I thought. Would I really be that disappointed? Is this still as good an idea as I once thought? I thought of my Matt. I wondered how he was feeling right now, knowing what was going to be happening. He hadn't texted me back, and I didn't blame him. How was I going to feel tomorrow? Tonight and tomorrow night are going to be intense. This is not something to take lightly, that's for sure.

I walked through the memories of our life together, Matt and me. I visited us on our wedding day. We were so young, so full of dreams. Looking back, feeling those feelings again made me look at myself as almost a different person. The chapters of our lives feel like someone has told you all about themselves, described everything so intensely that you almost created the memories and didn't actually experience them. Or that they are actually characters in a movie you saw once and really loved and remembered vividly. If only you could go back for one day to experience those days again. If only you'd appreciated those memories for what they were then, rather than looking forward so many years. People are planning and preparing for so many things all the time we forget to stop and love the moment, cherish the moment. I have so many friends, parties, memories I would give anything to revisit for just one day. To say hi. To tell them you are loving every stage with them before they move on. To tell them they mean something to you.

It made me recall one camping trip in my late teens with a group of friends. We'd stayed up all night drinking, laughing and talking by the campfire. There was only about six or seven of us. I remember the way the wilderness looked as dawn approached. I remember looking at the trees, at the sky, at the grass, and at my friends and not being able to breathe deeply enough. Time seemed to walk slowly by. I felt 'him' (Time) look at me as he walked and our eyes connected in a moment of almost divine connection. It was as if he was saying to me, *Can you see how lovely it is? Look how it is happening all around you. Thank you… thank you, Leola, for noticing, for loving this moment. I did it especially for you.* And as Time walked away I saw the world as I'd never perceived it before. It was alive, it was a small child waking on a Sunday morning, stretching in her footed pajamas, grinding her eyes with her small fists. And opening her eyes slowly, cautiously, she smiles into the eyes of her momma. Everywhere I looked was bathed in blue. It was breathtaking. It was magic, and it was especially for me. It lasted only a few moments before the sun vanquished the night sky and brightened everything the light touched.

I've never had the privilege of experiencing anything like that morning again in my life. Yes, I've had my children, and that was so special, but it was different special. That morning was only for me. I remember looking at my friends, thinking, *Are you seeing this, you guys?* But they were oblivious. They didn't notice what was happening around them. I can only hope they have a memory of their own that is as special.

Now today I will have another memory of my own. I will try to remember to stay in the moment, to not think about Matt, to not think about what will happen when this is over. Good, bad, or ugly I will experience this fully. But I have a feeling it will be nothing but the good.

There was a slight knock at the door. I froze on the bed, waiting for it to be followed with a sharp *Housekeeping!* but there was silence. Then, ever so quietly, I heard the card key slip into the lock and saw the door handle turn. I pushed play on my iPhone iPod. Then I stood up and smiled as Steve walked into the room. He closed the door and put the card key on the table by the door and stopped and looked at me. We stood like that in awkward silence for a moment, smiling like a couple of kids caught with their hands in the cookie jar.

"I was afraid you wouldn't come," he said and finally walked over to me.

I met him the last couple of steps as he wrapped me in his arms. I gave him a nice kiss full on the lips and hugged him.

"I was too," I lied.

"I like what you've done with the place," he said as he took off his coat. He placed it on the back of one of the chairs.

I unbuttoned my top. "Well thank you. I feel like it needed a woman's touch." I arched my eyebrow and smiled. "Would *you* like a woman's touch?"

He grabbed me around the waist and suctioned me to his middle. "Fuckin' right I would"—and just like that it began.

I couldn't get his shirt unbuttoned fast enough. He struggled with my tiny buttons so I switched and just undid my own top as he tackled his. With our shirts off, we clung to each other, his hand undoing my bra in the back as we fell onto the bed. *Fuck me* he was a great kisser. I explored his body—it was new, it was exciting. I briefly pictured Matt's hands exploring Emma's body, but when Steve bit my shoulder the vision exploded and I came back to the here and now. He was taller than Matt by a couple of inches, his shoulders wider.

We locked eyes and again I felt that familiar feeling with him. Perhaps a past life? He leaned in slowly and kissed me, my body enveloped in his arms. I felt so small and dainty and he touched me so. His kiss was firm but gentle. Not too soft, but more like that of a lover falling in love, so tender and sweet. He guided me slowly down to the bed, his arms so strong as he held me, his lips on mine, not wanting to miss a moment. Fuck was he good at that. I couldn't get enough. Tasting him. Tasting and memorizing the pout of his lips, the tracks of his teeth, and the soft hardness of his tongue.

We found our place on the bed, entangled, and our hands explored each other, every crevice. His hands toured my body, feeling every mound, every turn. Holy shit, it was so fucking hot. A new body. And it was all mine.

I leaned my head back and Steve moved into my neck. He sucked gently and bit me. My legs tingled. Exploring him, my hands found his cock, hard, so hard, and I guided it to my wet pussy. I was pulsing, waiting to feel him inside me. My hips raised and he guided it in, so gently. He wanted to feel every inch of me as well. I felt him slip inside of me, so wet. Every inch of his cock slowly moved inside. So fucking hot. I frantically grabbed his hips, trying to push him into me harder, faster, but he was strong and focused.

I looked at him and he was watching my face, his eyes so intent on mine. My heart was racing, sweat droplets gathered at my cleavage, and then he quickly pulled out. My breath caught and I dug my nails into his ass, begging him to go in again. His face didn't change as he started all over again. I felt like I was going to die with need. In and out, slowly I could feel every inch of his cock, he: feeling every crevice of my pussy. In and out. Over and over.

I clung to him, wrapping my legs around his back, forcing him to stay inside me. His breath washed over me, blanketing me with his desire. He fought my strong thighs and kissed me, crushing my lips to his. Then he fell on me and rammed me so hard my head hit the headboard. I didn't care, nor did he apologize. He fucked me hard; he couldn't hold back.

My legs wrapped around his back again, and I held on as he pumped and pumped. I grabbed his hair and pulled his head back, his eyes wild, crossed between pain and pleasure. Moaning and kissing, I clawed at him, bucking against him. I could feel it coming, could feel the tension. I squeezed his cock with my pussy and he cried out. I hooked my leg on him and flipped him onto his back. Sweat ran down my breasts and I didn't lose rhythm and I grinded my clit on him, his cock so deep inside. He grabbed my ass and dug his fingers in as his head arched back, exquisite pain on his face. Pumping madly, I rode him until we cried out together, juices running out of me down his balls and thighs. In the end, I collapsed on top of him, holding his face, and I fell beside him and he held me tight.

When he looked at me, he was crying. I was alarmed and asked him what was wrong. He wiped his tears and told me it was sweat and wiped them away and laughed. We lay like that in each other's arms for a while. The intensity of what happened slowly dimmed.

I thought of nothing but the two of us. I felt bad at how much I enjoyed it, but that was only a fleeting moment. I was doing this with my husband's permission and full knowledge. In the end, we'd decided to go without the video camera. We thought our own imagination at the storytelling would be better than hardcore, unedited, bad porn.

Exhausted, Steve and I lay beside each other, breathing in the sweaty air that blanketed beside us, falling like a heavy fog.

I propped up on my elbow and looked at him. "Holy fuck," I said.

Steve didn't answer. He just lay there smiling, breathing heavily. We lay like that for a few minutes. That was intense.

"So this is the deal, Mr. Steve," I began.

He begrudgingly propped up himself and smiled at me eager to hear what I had to say. "What's that, hot stuff?" he asked.

"Well, what I don't want is any after-fucking major cuddling or pillow talk. Minus today 'cause we have some rules to iron out. But what I don't want, at the same time, is the fuck-me-and-chuck me out the door scenario. You know? I mean, I know what we're doing is wrong, but I don't want to be made to feel like a cheap whore, either." I looked at him for affirmation.

"Deal. Let's say, what? No more than ten minutes of afterglow, and then be on our way?"

"That sounds about right," I agreed. "Enough time to catch our breath, maybe a few more nipple sucks, a couple more kisses, and we can head back to work!" I laughed as he dived for my nipples, expertly sucking them back and forth again.

"Stop or you're going to have to fuck me again, Mister!" He didn't stop right away and I wrapped my long legs around him and smothered his face in my breasts. He bear-hugged me and we lay like that for a moment, and then he lifted his head and kissed me again, longer than ever. The "it's over for today" kiss. Perfect. Then we got up, got dressed, and left the room, separately of course. He went first; I stayed to fix my hair and makeup. And then I headed straight home to shower.

17

I TEXTED MATT AS I walked to my car to head back to work. *Hi, babe… on my way home. xoxo*

Fucking weird to be texting my husband after he knows I was just with another man.

Hey!! how'd IT go? lol.

What a jackass. I wrote, *Fine. I can't wait to tell you all about it. When will you be home?*

I drove off. No "concert" this afternoon for me. I turned the radio to low and quietly sang some of my favorites, thinking of the afternoon and how I was going to explain to Matt what had happened. Do I tell him in point form? Do I tell him in a nonchalant, no-big-deal way? Or do I describe every detail, every feeling, a real "Shag 'n Brag" session…?

Bling! *Should be no more than an hour,* he wrote.

Good. I wanted to shower first. I felt dirty, especially for when the kids came home. I didn't want anything other than our safe, familiar smells on me for when I kissed my daughter.

I put in my Bluetooth and called Ever at a stop light. She answered before the first ring was done. "Hey, you fucking whore! Tell me every dirty detail!" she yelled at me.

"Fuck, Ever, aren't there people around you?" I scolded.

"Jesus, Lee, I told everyone; they're all waiting for the story too, so it's all good!"

My heart froze. *"No you did not,"* I threatened.

"Yeah I did. They're all dying within a few weeks anyway. It's all they have to get through the day, so spill it." She laughed, and I heard a chorus of laughter in the background. Ever was a palliative care nurse at the hospital. I had volunteered with her a couple of times. I thought I was going to throw up over my nerves, but she talks to patients with no filters and makes them blush and laugh and cringe all at the same time. Their families love her.

"Well, shit, Ever, why don't I just swing by and we can have circle time, maybe a picture book for those hard of hearing?" I snapped sarcastically.

"*Oh my God*, Leola, that would be amazing!"

"Shut up," I spat at her—with love. "Fine. I hope none of them jerk off later and have a heart attack and die. That'll be on your conscience, Ever."

"I would love that, actually. Put some of these poor bastards out of their misery," she said.

"You're going to hell." I laughed when I heard more cackles from the background. "Okay, here goes …" And I told her what happened, feeling a little guilty about telling her before Matt, but this was better anyway, giving me some practice before I had to tell it for real all too soon.

She thanked me for telling her and proceeded to inform me she hoped I knew what I was doing while I listened to a hundred-year-old voice in the background telling Ever to shut up and mind her own business.

I laughed and said good-bye as she wished me luck in sharing that *slice of pie* to Matt. *Not helping* .

Matt got home just after I fixed myself a cup of tea and had turned on the TV to kill time waiting for him. The kids wouldn't be home from school for another forty-five minutes, so we had time to talk this all out.

He came in, put his things right down, and grabbed a beer out of the fridge. He sat on the other side of the couch after he kissed me, took a pull on his beer, and looked at me.

"Okay! I'm ready!" he said honestly. His face was not upset;

he looked a little anxious, a little apprehensive, but I felt only good vibes. I hoped I felt like this tomorrow when I was on his end of the flaming sword. "Don't leave anything out. I want to hear what he was wearing, where he stood, what the room looked like, everything."

"I'll do my best. It's a lot for me to regurgitate. if you feel like I skipped over something, like I forget to say at what point I took off my shoes or something, just ask. I'm new at this, as you will be tomorrow, so just ask. I'm not *not* telling you anything if I don't tell you, okay? It's that I'm trying to not forget anything that I might forget something, you know?" I rambled.

"No worries, babe, I'll ask, I promise. And one other thing? Please look at me when you're telling me. There's nothing to be ashamed of, okay? I love you." He leaned over and kissed me again.

I nodded. Took a deep breath. Took stock of my emergency exits and hoped the air bags would deploy if summoned. And began.

When I finished describing to my husband my afternoon with another man, I sat for a moment with silence thick in the air between us. Matt had asked a few questions, but I felt like I did a pretty good job telling everything in the right order with the right amount of emphasis on the right parts. It was weird, fucking *weird* telling him this. Worse than descriptively telling your mother how you lost your virginity. Anyone done that? Yeah, I didn't think so. I reminded myself this was literally our first time doing this and it was okay that it was awkward.

"You okay?" I asked tentatively.

Matt took another pull at his beer. He nodded. "I'm good," he said. "Just need a moment."

I took this as an opportunity to make myself a stiff vodka and Sprite. I came back to the couch and sat with him.

"Well. I feel torn between being turned on and wanting to shoot myself in the face." He laughed. But not the good laugh. More like the I-can-feel–myself-edging-over-to–crazy-town kind of laugh.

"Really?" I asked. "You think more on the 'it turned me on' side though, babe?" I moved closer and ran my hand up his leg. "It sure turned me on telling you about it," I lied. I shouldn't say that …. While it was worse than awkward, with the right frame of mind for Matt it could really turn me on. I leaned in and kissed his neck, moving up to his ear and then to his mouth. "Maybe it turned you on just a teeny bit?" I breathed, striving for bravery.

He put his beer and my drink on the table. His mouth responded with pressure as he leaned me back onto the couch and laid me down. "Maybe just a *little*," he said. "Well… maybe just a little bit more," and with that he took me right on the couch. It was hard, eager, intense. He fucked me with complete abandon. I let him have his way with me. It was raw, rough, honest, and passionate, and I clung to him and let him drive into me again and again. He couldn't get deep enough. He drilled me into the couch for all it was worth. When he was spent, I held fast to him. There was nowhere I was going. I was right where I belonged.

We got up and dressed so as not to get caught by the kids coming home from school. I went to him and hugged him and kissed him and told him how much I loved him.

"I'm good, babe," he said, and he looked into my eyes. "Truly I am; I promise."

"Good, 'cause tomorrow, it's your turn," I said.

And my turn to be on the receiving end, I reminded myself. Dismissing the inevitable, we went about our night.

18

*C*HEAT: *TO DEFRAUD; SWINDLE; to deceive; influence by fraud; to elude; deprive of something expected.*
Used as a verb: to practice fraud or deceit; to violate rules or regulations.

Steve and Emma were cheating on each other, but wouldn't that mean Matt and I were "cheating" on Steve and Emma as well? We were being deceitful, taking something that wasn't ours behind their backs. It was interesting.

So here I was the following morning at work. I couldn't concentrate because I had the anticipation of Matt and Emma that afternoon, and Ever was away on a mini-vacation for the weekend. *This is going to drive me to drink.* I pretended to do work. I opened my e-mails and stared unseeing at my screen for ten minutes, opened my Facebook page and perused through the statuses until I'd read them all but had no idea what anyone was doing, and I eventually stared at my phone texts. I decided to delete the text thread from Steve in case my daughter ever happened upon them. I sat at my desk staring at the walls.

I briefly contemplated redecorating my room, maybe moving some things around on the shelves when my phone beeped with a text.

Hi, honey. How are you holding up? Matt wrote.

Bless his soul. *Super Dee Dooper, babe! lol. Heard anything yet?*

I did. we're meeting at 2. You good?

Oh yeah! I'm peachy! *I'm good, babe. Have fun! Love you xox*

Okay, here it goes. Well, I'd had a fantastic morning, so the afternoon should be smooth sailing as well! I ruefully thought.

Fuck this shit. I locked my computer and left Cassie a note that I would be on my cell if she needed me. I sent a text to Ever that she was a terrible friend for leaving me during my time of need and went to an afternoon flick by myself. That would definitely help pass the time.

It worked like a charm! I'd texted Matt to let him know I would be at the movies for the afternoon and I would answer any of his texts when the movie was over. I thoroughly enjoyed the movie, and it kept me from going crazy watching the clock. The time it took for popcorn, the upcoming trailers, and the movie itself was long enough to bring me out the other side knowing Matt and Emma would be done. When the show was over, there was a text from Cassie: *Sounds good,* and one from Ever: *Bite me,* and one from Matt about forty-five minutes before: *Hey, love. I'll be home soon.*

I don't remember the drive.

19

*I*CAN DO THIS! I gave myself the little-engine-that-could pep-talk as I sat in my car in the driveway. If Matt could do it, so could I. I checked my teeth in the rear-view mirror and heaved my thousand-pound body out of the car. I used superhuman strength to walk one anvil-coated foot after the other to the front door. My head felt awkward on my neck. Why did it feel like my ear lobes were touching my shoulders and my hair was standing straight up in all directions?

I looked at my reflection in the window of our living room as I walked to the front door to see what was going on with my head. Although it *looked* normal, I could tell I was only seeing what I wanted to see.

In actuality, I was a Ronald McDonald hairdo on top of a Jack in the Box head with cow vaginas for ears. It was *not* amusing. My breasts were missing and my arms and hands were monkey-long and hairy. *I can't possibly face Matt looking like this.* I looked back to the car contemplating my escape. Then I realized I would never fit back in with this oddly shaped body, never mind picturing a cop's reaction when he pulled me over. I would be on the news, hauled off to some scientific lab where they would anal probe me trying to figure out what kind of alien had abducted me and took me apart just to put me together with different configurations of our earthly bounty for shits and giggles.

No, I will just go inside. I can do this.

I watched myself open the front door and walk into a carbon copy of my home. Everything was in the same place as in my own home. I couldn't hear the shower, but Matt's truck was in the driveway, so I knew he was home. Assuming he was done with the shower, I watched myself walk down the hall to my bedroom's twin. I wished it was like a dream, where you're trying to get to the end of the hallway but the door stays just out of reach. Unfortunately, stupid reality got in the way of this nightmare, and the stupid bedroom door was inches in front of me within seconds. Stupid Matt was inside the stupid room.

Taking a deep breath, I watched my hand grasp the handle and turn the knob, and I walked in. "Hi babe..."

Matt came right over to me, took one look at me, and pulled me into his arms. I fell against him, sucking every fiber of his being to fill me with strength. I knew everything was going to be okay.

He pulled away after a minute and gave me a big kiss. "How are you?" he asked, real concern filling his eyes.

Crap, he'd noticed the cow vagina ears. "I'm good. Just breathing. I don't know how you did this yesterday, babe!" I cried, breaking out a brave smile for good measure.

"I don't know either!" He laughed. "But you know what, my sweet love?"

I looked at him doubtfully.

"Once you and I started talking, it got better and better by the minute." He took my hand, and we went to the bed and lay down beside each other. "Are you ready?" he asked.

I leaned in for one more kiss. I smiled. *The little engine that could!* "Go. I'm ready."

"So," he began. "She was already there when I got to the room. I was so nervous, babe. She was sitting on the bed when I walked in. She was wearing a white lingerie top with little panties, bare feet. I went to her and gave her a hug and a kiss, pretending to be brave. We talked for a few minutes; I can't even remember what we talked about, just stupid things like, *How long have you been waiting* stuff like that." He stopped. "Remember to ask me questions if you feel like I'm leaving anything out 'cause I'm really nervous right now, okay?" I nodded. "I think it'll get better as we get better at this, you know?"

"It's all good, babe, no worries, okay?" I kissed him softly and patted his hand—*you're a trooper!* "Go on," I urged.

"Okay. So we started kissing, and I—" He smiled anxiously at me. He looked like a terrified little boy.

Leaning in, I kissed his neck and whispered, "Keep going." I ran my hand up and down his arm, over his hips, kissing his chest. "It's okay," I promised. I felt like I was going to barf.

Distracted, now with his hands on me, rubbing me the same way I was rubbing him, he continued. "I guided her onto the bed, laid her down, and took off my shirt. Then I climbed on top of her and we kissed. She's a good kisser, like you said Steve was. She was good at that. We kissed and explored each other with our hands. I slid her panties down while she scooched up the bed to give me room to lie down. I went down on her—and babe, it was good."

My breath caught, but I pushed through it. I don't even think Matt noticed. "She tasted good. Then she traded places with me, and I took the rest of my clothes off and she gave me head." He looked at me straight on. "She's not as good as you, though," he reassured me. *Good boy.* "She only did it for a few minutes; I think she knew that for our first time, I wasn't going to last long. We made out some more and then I rode her. It turns out I didn't last as long as I'd like to've. She didn't cum, though. When I was done I went down on her again to finish her off. Then we lay together for a few minutes, same as you and Steve, and talked about the same stuff you talked to Steve about. She didn't play any music like you did, though. I liked that you did that, I wish she had, too. Maybe I'll do it next time."

He looked at me. It felt like he'd said the whole thing in one breath. "How'd I do?"

Letting go of the air I didn't realize I was holding, I smiled at him. Poor thing, he was like a spider—more afraid of me than

I was of him. "You did really great, actually." I reassured him. "And you're right, that was easier as you went along. It was like hearing a fantasy of yours, but knowing it's true. And it was pretty fucking hot, if I'm going to be honest!"

Laughing, he pulled me close and kissed me deep and strong, and I responded and proceeded to take my clothes off and ride him like he'd never been ridden before.

When we were done, we just looked at each other with shit-eating grins. "How fucked up are we?" I blurted. "I mean, really... Who does this? This is *crazy*!" We laughed so hard. Pillows were punched, blankets were thrown, and we tickled and laughed and grabbed and it was a frenzy of nerves and laughter that shook all the anxiety out. *Fuck it—let's just do this.*

I *had* to admit; as much as I wanted to barf, I was glad this first time was done with. The virginity had been taken, the cherry popped, we were over the worst of it, and it was smooth sailing from then on in. There was no turning back now, right? We had to jump in with both feet.

We were going to redefine relationships. Oprah was going to want to interview us! Dr. Phil was going to have us on his show sharing with the world how we revolutionized marriages! No, not really. People are way too set in their ways; people are way too scared to try stuff like this. And for the most part, relationships are too damaged to experiment with something like this. Either damaged from previous relationships or ruined from their own internal course, this kind of thing is reserved for a) fucked up people such as ourselves (*best people ever*); or b) people who are bored shitless in their relationships.

The "sanctity" of marriage will prevail for the masses. And that's okay. More for me! I feel like one day, like maybe in the year 4012, they will be reading about Matt and Leola and how we were the pioneers of this newly revolutionized way of marriage. Maybe I'd come up with the answer to it all! Not the secretly making-couples-cheat-on-each-other part, of course.

No? Ah well, to each their own...

20

TO SAY THIS HAD captivated my life would be an understatement. It was hard not to think about it all the time. Being a mother, a career woman, a friend, a wife all the while trying to live this secret life from everyone you know and love except your partner is exhausting. I couldn't talk to anyone about it until Ever came back and the waiting drove me nuts. It's nice to have this secret with Matt, but I'm a girl and girls need their girlfriends to talk and dissect and talk and turn things over and over and over until it's been all talked through. It sucks that I couldn't do that. At least she'd be back soon. Just not soon enough. I wished I had other close girlfriends to talk about it to. Get different perspectives.

I was soon going to be driven to having an imaginary friend.

Steve texted me a few times over the weekend, once to touch base—*such chivalry*—and a couple times to tell me he was thinking of me and couldn't wait to do it again if I was so inclined—*uh, yes, please*.

I showed Matt all the texts and encouraged him to make sure he reached out to Emma as well. He mirrored Steve's texts using his own words; it was nice to have Steve's texts as reference points. The funny thing was, Emma's texts back were *not* very "good girl." They were so funny. *You rocked my fucking world,*

Matt... we need to do that again very soon! And, *You make me so wet, I am counting down the days!*

With that as an invitation, Matt and I upped our text play with both of them.

When Ever came back from her weekend in New York, she wanted to know everything. We met Monday night for a drink at the pub and she was there before me, which disappointed me (I like to watch her arrival and the reaction of the men in the bar). My drink was already ordered and on the table when I walked in. Her face stalked me as I maneuvered through the tables to the back corner, our favorite perch so we could watch the whole bar. On this night, however, her eyes were trained on me.

It was odd how she wanted to hear every detail, every plan, but she was so against it and wasn't afraid to speak her mind. "You guys are insane!" she declared, slamming a hand on the table.

I looked at her while smiling because I know my best friend and her declarations.

She sat back, picked up her drink, and swallowed. "I don't know what the hell I'm listening to! You guys are crazy!" She looked at me for answers.

I had none. "I know, Ever, trust me, I know. It's crazy! There's nothing else to say!" I agreed.

We laughed together in an uncomfortable moment at the sheer asinine conversation we were having. My fifteen-year-old self would have been in shock. (*You signed us up for* what?) "You're just jealous," I threw out.

"*What? You* are smoking some potent shit, darling. There's no fucking way I'm jealous of this. You guys are a freight train heading to Crashville," she predicted. "No way in hell I'm jealous. Clint would have a heart attack if any chick touched him like that!" We laughed. "Fuck, that man wouldn't know *what* to fucking do. The poor girl would up and leave him lying there in a pool of his own premature ejaculation!"

Ever and I laughed so hard people were looking at us.

"He'd probably fart trying to bend over to eat her out!" I

shrieked. I thought Ever was going to die laughing. Tears streamed down my face as I tried to catch my breath to talk. "'Oh, I'm sorry, babe,'" I mocked Clint, "'it's okay, it doesn't stink.'"

Ever whooped and slammed the table. "'Munch munch!'" she cried. "'Okay, all done! What? I know it was only thirty seconds, but it's *my* turn,'" in perfect Clint mode, and then proceeded to spank the air like some club dancer. The waitress came over to bring us new drinks and smiled politely at our obvious comedic talents.

"Sorry to interrupt," she said as she placed our glasses down and took our empty ones. "Here are some napkins; looks like you'll need them."

"Thank you," I said as I took one and wiped my eyes. When she left, I leaned over the table and scolded Ever. "Poor Clint. It can't be that bad."

"Yeah? Okay then, Mrs. I'm Married to a Hottie. Whatever you say," she said as she too grabbed a napkin. I stuck my tongue out at her. "All I'm saying is Clint would never be up for anything like this and neither would I. I'm not giving some bitch full rein with my husband, whether he's hot or not," she stated and took a drink. "Matt is fucking hot! You're playing a dangerous game. Some chick is going to steal him from you, mark my words. I would steal him for fuck's sake!"

I laughed.

"I'm serious! Now... that does *NOT* mean that I don't want to hear every dirty fucking detail, though. okay?"

"Yeah, yeah. ALL right. Fine. I'll be careful!" I insisted. She looked at me doubtfully. "I *will*," I pushed. "It'll be fine. Let's change the subject. How was New York? I can't believe you got Clint to go there with you. That's crazy; doesn't seem much like his thing."

"I didn't go with Clint I went with a girlfriend. We went to a hair conference thing, and it was really great. We went to Ground Zero too. It was amazing. Too big for anyone to take in, really," she said quickly and then paused. "Even though I don't have any personal ties to it, just *being* there is overwhelming. The power in the air is tangible, you know?" She looked at me. "There's nothing to do but take in what you can and give back what you can. It was intense."

"I'll bet," I agreed. "One day I'll make it there. I feel like it's a place for giving and receiving love, exchanging it, and recycling it back and forth to anyone and everyone who comes there. The air must be thick with it?"

"Yes, it was totally like that. Pretty fucking crazy, that's for sure! Anyway, it was a nice weekend, weather was great, and I learned lots about hair!"

We chatted about the kids and work and then parted ways.

Matt came up with a great idea and I couldn't help but get excited. After all, I didn't want to run the whole show (*let's be honest—yes I did*), but it's nice when he takes some initiative so I don't have to be the bad guy the whole time. After all, if this all goes to shit, I'll be supremely pissed off if I don't have anything to throw in *his* face!

He wanted to plan a night out with the four of us. Because when we first met, it was the four of us. Now with this having happened last week, we hadn't made anymore plans. Of course, if nothing was going on behind closed doors, we would all hang out together; after all, we'd just met and we all liked each other. We had to keep that going or they were going to get suspicious. So I had to text Steve and Matt had to text Emma and point this out. (You don't want to get your wife/husband suspicious, do you? Why all of a sudden are we not hanging out, same goes for us, with my wife/husband.) I couldn't believe I hadn't thought of this. That could really have fucked everything up.

That day, I got a text from Emma saying she was so sorry she hadn't texted in a while, been busy for a while there but would love to get together the next night at a bar for a few drinks. I told her that would be perfect and we'd meet them at The Hub at 8:30 tomorrow night.

There were starting to be way too many firsts. It was like everything was being felt with a heightened sensitivity. Like when you have your first baby, you notice everything. I couldn't wait for this stage to be over with. Unlike with your first baby, I wanted this to be my third baby, the one who almost diapers himself at six months because you're too busy to get to the poor thing. It was so stressful, anticipating meeting them. I knew the basics: go to Emma first, hugs and kisses, then over to Steve—don't make it too awkward (*I am breezy*)—and then… what? Do I sit beside Matt across from Steve, or would that be wrong? Or do I sit across from Emma? *Is that too obvious that I'm avoiding Steve?* I needed a drink *stat*.

In the end, Matt and I decided to try to get there first and let Steve and Emma stress about it.

When we got to the bar, the bastards were already there. *Shitballs.* Big hugs, smiles, and kisses were showered all around, and in the end we were sitting at a round table—*are you kidding me?*—and it was boy-girl all the way around. But it ended up working out.

Crossing my legs back and forth, I traded between touching Matt's leg and Steve's, and I thoroughly enjoyed myself. (*Again, I'm going to hell; yes I acknowledge this. At least I admit it.*)

Steve and Emma were casual and talkative and animated and fun. Perhaps they've done this before? I felt as if I was see-through and everyone was watching my thoughts live on TV.

In the end, I felt like we were victorious and gained some confidence. And it was fun having this secret, this multifaceted secret. There were so many layers to weave through. For Matt and me. For Steve and me. For Matt and Emma. For me and Emma—not to be confused with Emma and me or the same for Matt and Steve. It was almost too much, and I felt like I'd swallowed a coat hanger; my cheeks were hurting halfway through the night from so much smiling. I was thoroughly enjoying myself at the pleasure of having this power.

Don't we all want that at some point with someone or something in our lives? It felt like the best Christmas ever, with Santa in the room, your children looking at him with magic in their eyes. My heart soared with elation.

Unfortunately, the only way from here is down...

21

WITH THIS NEWFOUND INNER demon awakened in us, we decided to extend our interests to other venues to try to attract some fresh meat. I was like a lioness in heat, foaming at the mouth for the strongest alpha male. Matt like a peacock, strutting around showing off his feathers for the finest female. We were high on our own pheromones, on the lookout at all times. Steve and Emma were amazing; we were meeting up almost once a week with them. But we wanted more.

We started with online searches. We went on dating sites and on the cheat-on-your-spouse sites. Wow, what a lot of work for a lot of disappointment. We were surprised at how many people were signed up on these websites. How responsible, though, if you think about it. These people were looking for specific qualities; of the most important were full secrecy and no crazy woman or man expecting the other to leave his or her spouse. At least they were honest with the other person, but that doesn't negate the fact that they were lying to their spouse...

Unfortunately, the weird and way-too-out-there-for-us far outweighed the good. Here's a small taste of what we were up against:

Bachelor #1: Jim is looking for a dominatrix who wants to get together for kink and S&M. He is very happily married, but his wife is not interested in any fetishes and he doesn't want her to leave him, so he's been living with this secret. *Next!*

Bachelor #2: Paul is looking for a woman who will fulfill his fantasy of strap-on sex. He's gay but enjoys the strap-on with a woman, as they are softer. His partner is revolted by women, however, which is why he is looking for this on the side. *Next next!*

Bachelor #3: Troy is looking for a woman who doesn't care so much about looks and would be interested in showing him around town, as he is new. No hanky panky, just a friend unless something happens to "come up." His wife has not moved here yet; she is finishing her schooling and will join him in the summer. Until then, he would like some companionship. *No, thanks.*

Bachelor #4: Arj is looking for hot women to fuck whenever they want. His wife is pregnant and not very compliant at the moment and he needs more. *Hmmm. Let's see a picture and we'll talk…*

Bachelorette #1: Sabrina is looking for a man who will be "so romantic" with her. Her husband is wonderful, but they've been together so long and the passion has been in a rut for the last few years. She needs to feel like a woman again. *Not bad…*

Bachelorette #2: Julie is looking for a rich man to shower her with gifts and for hot sex whenever he wants it as long as he buys her beautiful things and is nice to her. *Next!*

Bachelorette #3: Anya would like you to know she is single and very pregnant and wants to get her rocks off before the baby is born, so if you're interested, please "get in touch"! *Uhhh next!*

Perhaps that was not the best way to go about it. Instead, we thought maybe the sites you have to pay for would be worth the trial period. The only glitch with this plan was it was individual people. We wanted to do this with couples. I don't know why; it's just how we felt. Maybe we were like relationship counselors, educating couples showing them the way to go… *I don't know anything. I'm making shit up.* We liked the couple thing because it felt more like we were in this together.

So after a lot of discussion, Matt and I decided to stick with meeting real people. The websites are filled with couples meeting couples; married woman looking for fun; married man looking for fun; singles looking for singles; or couples looking for a single for threesomes; etc. There's nothing about what we were looking for because there is *no* way to advertise what we were looking for. We were an anomaly, and the only way to solve an anomaly is to find information where there is none to be found. And we were hoping no information would ever be found.

When I was in college, I met a boy (*shocking, I know*). He was my first real love. We've all had love in high school; well, some people do, anyway. I had crushes and infatuations but no real love. When I first started college, I'd gone out with a few boys but I was so nervous, naïve, so deer-in-the-headlights that I didn't do very well. I didn't handle school, dating, and living on my own for the first time as much as I would like to have. It was daunting, and it was a lot for me to balance. Looking back, I just wasn't ready.

One guy I went out with one time—his name was Beck (short for some last name I can't recall)—was nice enough but after a couple of hours of hanging out, I knew there was nothing there. And just before the date was over, this other guy came into the coffee shop, waved a hello to Beck and went to the counter. Intuitively I knew this man would be mine. I didn't want to ask Beck who this guy was, I just wanted to end the date as soon as possible. But he delayed and I missed following this new guy to introduce myself. I'd abruptly ended communication with Beck hoping he'd get the hint, which he did.

And then, about 2 weeks later, I saw Beck's friend again. We must have had the same spare because he started to come in with a group of friends to one of the quiet areas of the college called The Met at the same time as me. I went to eat and read late every morning by myself after my second class to get away and have some Leola time. When I saw him again I almost fell over the back of one of the soft, cushy chairs. So embarrassing. We didn't speak to each other for the first time for nearly three weeks after that, but we always made eye contact, and he smiled every time I came in. I felt him watch me sit down, and I always sat facing him, turned slightly to the side so it wasn't obvious. I thought I saw Beck come in a few times and hung out with the group, but this new boy had taken my heart at first sight. I guess Beck had noticed that. He'd never bothered me again.

I remember that first time Blake came over to me; he had on worn-out jeans, Converse sneakers, and a plaid shirt with the sleeves folded partway up his arm. His dark-brown, shaggy hair was flipped with soft curls around the bottom.

It was so distracting to look into his brown eyes when I realized he was coming over. I had planned for so long what I would say to him when I finally got the nerve to approach him. Now that he was coming over to me, I'd frozen on the spot, and the only thing I could come up with was a lame, "Hi." My heart sank into my stomach, and it felt like an eternity before he'd responded. The best part was, he'd frozen on the spot too and could only come up with a "Hey." He sat there for 472 hours—*I swear it was that long*—before he handed me a piece of paper and got up and walked away. It was his name and phone number. I felt like I was floating out on a cloud. I immediately loved him.

I called Blake that night and every night after that for eight months. Then we'd spent the summer together in his truck, traveling the country, camping all over, hiking trails, and living life in a dream. We met the coolest people, we sang while we drove, we were summer gypsies, and I knew I was going to marry this man. He was the reason I was alive.

Thanksgiving in my second year, we both went home to our families. I'd met his family that summer and he'd met mine on spring break. We thought it would be important for us to have some time with them alone that year as we'd been gone all summer and then back to school, so we didn't want to take away this important holiday, especially since we were planning on going to Mexico for Christmas and New Year's. We thought if we did Thanksgiving, perhaps it would be an easier pill for them to swallow. Spending even those three days away from him felt like a life sentence, but I knew Blake and I would have forever together, so I sucked it up.

We'd spent the morning together; I drank in his essence as much as I could. I had a crush on this man, I was infatuated with him and was madly, fiercely in love. I wondered when he would ask me to marry him already. But it really didn't matter. He was mine forever; there was no rushing anything. We talked, we laughed, and we packed. And we made sweet love until we had to pull ourselves out of each other's embrace, and then we kissed one last time good-bye.

Nine hours later, my world ended.

The phone rang at my parents' house at 10:43 p.m. I don't know why I know that. My mother answered the phone, and then her face fell as she looked at me. I felt my insides turn to ice and my face lose all sensation. And then the world spun the wrong way as she hung up the phone and came to me.

I don't remember anything she said. I only remember feeling like I was dying. I couldn't breathe. I couldn't see. I remember thinking, *Where is this bright light you're supposed to see?* at the same time the terror rose inside me and told me, *There is no light... you are not dead... but you are in hell.*

And I was. I was in actual Hell. Capital H. It's still so hard to talk about to this day. I couldn't move for five months. I remember very little. He'd been my life. He was my best friend. Matt doesn't know about him. Blake is mine, and I keep him in a special place in my heart. A place where no one else is invited. I shut down for almost two years. During that time, I'd dropped out of college—I couldn't bear to go—everywhere I went I expected to see Blake. When I finally started to allow myself to heal, I'd enrolled in real estate courses. That's when I met Matt, and I felt like I could have a chance at this happiness thing again. Of course, it would never be the same, but I believed it could be close. And I was right.

﹀

About two years ago my father broke his foot, and on his first weekend of being an invalid (*you* know men), my mother came down with the flu, so I went home and spent the weekend with them, cleaned the house, got them stocked up on groceries, and made a few dinners to store in the freezer.

On my way out to the car at the grocery store one day, I ran into a few of the guys from college and stopped to say hi. They were friendly enough, although a couple of them were weird, and some I didn't recognize. It was an awkward blip in my day as I quickly briefed them with a general overview of my life: married, two kids, a realtor living in Long Beach, etc. Some threw me kind words—a few of the others kept to themselves—and one hung in for the conversation but kept his head down and then rudely turned away as we all parted ways.

Seeing those guys in my hometown had been a tough day for me. That night I dug out all my pictures of Blake's and my year together. I sat in the basement where I could be alone after I put my parents to bed and cried and sobbed and laughed and fell apart as the pathetic scrap of a patch I'd attempted to mend my broken heart with disintegrated. With a gaping hole in my soul, I compiled my pictures in chronological order and put together a computer file of our life on disk so I could watch it whenever I wanted. Complete with music, I tortured myself over and over again until I fell asleep from exhaustion.

So when I saw Blake at my favorite coffee place one morning, you can imagine my reaction. I grasped on to reality with both hands and fought insanity in a duel to the death.

22

HAVE YOU EVER SEEN a ghost? I haven't, but I can imagine the first time anyone sees one, there's a universal reaction. No matter your culture, your country, whether male or female, young or old, I would imagine it would all be pretty similar. All your blood drops instantly to your feet and is immediately replaced with adrenaline. Your heart enlarges ten times, as do your eyes, which quickly look away and then look back. Your ears don't work; it sounds as if you are on the bottom of a pool. In the meantime, your brain is computing everything at once, and at the same time it cannot make sense of what it's seeing. Time stops. Then you realize you're not breathing as everything rushes back to normal, sounds start coming back, your eyes finally blink, and everything around you starts moving again.

As I looked at Blake, my heart broke again. Physically broke right there in the middle of the coffee shop. I reached for the counter to steady myself. Of course it wasn't him. He looked at me and my breath caught. I knew it wasn't him. But Blake was all I could see.

When he left, I sat at one of the bistro tables by the wall and breathed. My coffee sat on the multicolored mosaic table while I concentrated on reality and the sounds of busy, white-collared people faded to a low hum. I think about Blake often. The memories usually make me cry. Alone I walk through my past, holding hands with my feelings, conversing with my subconscious, and playing with the souvenirs of my soul. More often than not I will play songs that take me back to those times. They are my lullaby, to send the memories back to sleep for a time, waiting for me to invite them out again to play.

I suddenly looked up, realizing I couldn't let him leave me again. I grabbed my coffee and ran out the door, looking up and down the street trying to spot him, to no avail. I strained to see him through the sea of people. I knew he was gone. What was I going to say to him anyway? *Hey, do you know you look like my boyfriend who died twenty years ago?* "Uh, okay, creepy old lady."

It was better he was gone.

Defeated, I walked back to the office and contemplated pouring a stiff one. It was five o'clock somewhere…

Cassie greeted me with a sour look when I got back to the office. Not in the mood to ask her what was up, I nodded a mirrored expression. Understanding, she nodded back, gave me a salute, and went back to work. I was so lucky to have her; she just "gets it," and one day I should tell her how much that means to me.

As per my usual routine, when I needed to soothe that broken part, I inserted into my computer the flash drive that I kept saved in my drawer marked Cassie's Old Files. I figured if anything happened to me, anyone going through my desk would see that and just hand it to Cassie without looking at its contents. Cassie would of course be confused and watch it. And she would understand and she would keep it away from Matt or anyone who would be hurt by it.

With the door to my office already closed, I turned the volume on low and watched the slideshow I'd painfully put together years ago. I'd agonized over the song to play it to, finally settling on "Just the Way You Are" by Billy Joel. I don't know why I continually do this to myself. I felt like an alcoholic falling off the wagon each time. Tears fell, and I absently wiped them away as I watched through smiling eyes my summer with Blake. We'd taken so many pictures.

Fifty percent of them were Blake and me, with my arm stretched out in front of us so you could only see part of my arm as I took all those self-portraits. We were alone for so much, there had been no one to take the pictures for us. There were pictures of us driving in our beat-up Honda Civic. We'd traveled everywhere in that thing. And we were packed from floor to roof. I'd sifted through all the scenery pictures for this particular project. I only included a few here and there; the rest were of us making funny faces or posing silly in front of landmarks. My favorites were the ones I took of us kissing, the two of us off-center as I clamored to get us both in the photo. Holding the camera at odd angles. Half of them were of us laughing or singing. Oh, my heart!

I try to figure out so often why he'd come into my life. Why had he, other than teach me how to love, how to receive love and ultimately, how to live even though I wanted to die? What purpose did that serve...?

Fuck Blake's frozen-in-time twin. I just hated when I got like this. It's so painful and it was so long ago! *Get over it already, Leola,* I scolded myself. I watched for a few more minutes and then pressed stop before it was over. Wiping the last of the tears away, I put the flash drive back into my desk drawer and called Ever.

"Please tell me you're not working today," I begged. There was silence. She knew me well enough when she heard a certain tone in my voice that I was having a bad 'Blake' day. I'd never told her about my file or that I torture myself on a semi regular basis with it. But she knew about Blake and that some days I break. She knew that sometimes I just needed her. I needed her to figure out her shit for the moment and drop everything to be there for me. It was embarrassing and I felt weak and don't want to have to explain or defend myself. I just need her then.

"No, I'm not working," was all she said. Even if she was working, she'd lie and go into a room where she could talk to me privately. She would be there for me. Fuck I loved this woman.

"I was at a coffee shop." I started bawling into the phone, quietly so Cassie wouldn't hear me.

"It's okay." She shushed me gently. "It's okay."

"Blake was there!" I cried. "I swear I saw him. It was exactly him." I held the phone in one hand while my other hand held my head. "He looked at me and smiled, Ever. It was exactly him. Like his twin but the same age as when he died. Oh my God." I took a deep breath. Ever was quiet, letting me talk. "I froze. I couldn't move. And then he just walked out like he had somewhere to fucking go!"

"That's crazy," she said. "Wow. Are you okay?"

"I don't know. That's the thing. What the fuck just happened? Was he a ghost? Am I losing my mind? Is this whole Steve and Emma thing putting me over the edge? Or did I just see what I think I saw? Of course it wasn't him. *Of course it wasn't him*," I emphasized with complete devastation. "But then what the *fuck*! Crazy. It's crazy!"

"Totally. That's totally crazy. You *know* Blake is dead. It's just a look-a-like, Lee," she said gently. "The differences are there, you just didn't see him long enough to notice," she suggested.

"You're right. Okay. You're right." I held my hand over my mouth in disbelief, still trying to put it all together. "I know he's dead," I managed to choke out. "This guy just looked exactly like him. It was scary. But yes, you are right. Thanks for talking me down." And as I ended the call, I felt confidence filing me again. *I'm not crazy*, I told myself. But even still, I wanted to see him again. I just really wanted to pretend, if only for a moment, that he was still alive.

23

KEEPING UP APPEARANCES BECAME important. Matt and Emma and Steve and I kept the texts coming and the meetings frequent. Matt and I tried to keep the sexual encounters to between once a week and a week and a half. After the initial losing of our cherries in sharing our first sexual encounter, our "shag 'n brag" sessions became something we looked forward to. Actually, more often than not, the "brag" part was almost our favorite. We touched each other during these sessions, exploring each other with new sensations as we listened and talked. Like new lovers our skin felt more sensitive; each crevice became new again. It was exciting. Matt and I made sure to make plans for the four of us about twice a month. I made sure I paid lots of attention to Emma when we were all out together, knowing she felt powerful thinking I knew nothing. And I made sure I paid lots of attention to Steve, loving the power I felt knowing Emma thought she was on top of the world. It was so wrong. And my nipples stood at attention saluting me with respect at the sheer knowledge of it all, waiting for their next command.

Let me tell you a few things about Steve that I cannot tell my husband but could tell Ever. I have never seen a nicer penis. I mean, I think all penises are hot. For the most part, anyway. I don't think I've seen an ugly penis, but there are the slightly curved-to-the-side ones, the too-dark-pubic-hair ones, the foreskin ones (I'm fine with the look of them; don't think they're ugly by any means. They're just different and not common so not familiar), the too big or too small of a head in relation to the shaft ratio, and the too big or too small balls. That said, they are all attractive to me; I just love them all.

But Steve's is perfection. Perfect head-to-shaft ratio, perfect color of pubic hair that is *well* maintained (yes, boys, it's not just important for girls), and the perfect-sized balls. Incredible, really. So perfect, in fact, that I named his penis 'Perfecto'.

Next on the list: he has stamina! He can go and go and go and go. The control he has is impressive.

Did I mention his gorgeous cock?

And last: he can make me squirt. I *know* we are supposed to share everything, but I can't tell Matt these things. We are in this to enjoy it *with* each other, and I really see no point in sharing such details with him. It would only hurt his feelings. What I plan on doing, however, is coming up with a night where Matt "tries" to make me squirt and succeeds. And we can celebrate together, and then I can tell him that ever since he got me to squirt, it must've opened up something in me and so now it has happened with Steve and we can enjoy that part together. Then I can have my cake and eat it too.

Matt's rendezvous with Emma have been quite steamy, if I'm to be honest. She's into the role-playing, dressing the part and playing it up. Matt and I never got into role-playing, mostly because of me, I guess. He seemed to enjoy it with Emma, though. She does all the dressing, all the decorating of the room, stuff like that. He gets into the role-playing with her verbally, so he says. Matt had shared with me parts they had played, the lonely housewife and mailman or pizza boy, and cops and robbers, just to name a few. I have to admit I enjoy hearing about it, though I could never do it myself. I just never got into that whole genre of sex.

The one downfall with this whole thing is the personal details we became privy to. Matt and I started to get to know Steve and Emma's relationship more than I think they knew their relationship. From what Steve told me and Emma told Matt, we truly knew everything, even the things they couldn't share with each other. We learned they didn't communicate with each other very well. Matt and I discussed what we could and should do with this information. Truly, we could destroy this marriage or save it. Depending on what our moods were, we truly were the judge and jury, and they didn't even know they were on trial. Although I loved the power that came with this position, I didn't want to play God in someone else's relationship. We decided to keep the information to ourselves for a while, until or if we needed it.

Ever thought that was the best part of the whole fucking thing. The power, the knowledge that at any moment we could seriously fuck up someone's life. "I am a sadist and I own it," she admitted. "How can you not love that? If this whole thing goes to shit for you and Matt, at least you'll know you could have your revenge. It would be all you have!" she rationalized.

Very true, I agreed.

Three weeks after I saw "Blake," I saw him again in the same coffee shop I hadn't missed a morning in since my first sighting. I went in every day and sat at one of the tables by the wall, the same table I had tangled tongues with reality all those weeks ago. Insanity and I had gotten to know each other intimately that day. Always better to keep your friends close and your enemies closer, as the saying goes.

Every customer who entered the coffee shop brought my head up hopefully, only to be disappointed each time. But then, finally, after three weeks, he walked in again. I saw Blake's eyes, his mannerisms, the way he walked. Everything. At first my soul soared with elation. Then I was filled with devastation when I realized the pain would never go away. I watched him order a coffee, get his money out of his jeans, and wait for his coffee, reading the chalkboard menu in the mom-and-pop coffee shop while they made his coffee.

Our eyes met, and I summoned superhero strength to hold his gaze for a moment as I forced a playful smile to slowly form on my face. His face mirrored mine as a perfect smile crept across his face. I looked down, still smiling, and picked up my coffee to my lips.

When I looked back, he was turning around, thanking the lady behind the counter as she handed him his coffee. As he walked past me, we looked at each other and said, "Morning." And then he was gone.

Watching him leave, my face reflected my mood and smiling, I slowly finished reading the paper before heading off to work. I called Ever but she didn't answer, so I left her a message. I told her I'd finally seen that guy at the coffee shop again and that she had been right. It wasn't Blake, and on closer inspection, he did in fact look different. I don't know why I lied to her; she would never judge me. I think it was because I needed to keep this for myself. For my heart. For my soul to heal. This big of a thing I needed to keep private. If I was losing my mind, I didn't want any spectators.

I decided later that morning to make an impromptu visit to Matt. I texted my husband, and to his surprise, we met that afternoon at a hotel room for some afternoon delight. I felt the universe was trying to tell me something, and although I didn't know what it was, it seemed important to remember what some good old-fashioned sneaking around with your husband could do for your relationship.

24

I'M NOT GOING TO try to pretend to anyone that this was easy. While Matt and I had so much fun, had this freedom to sleep with someone else, there were a lot of things we hadn't anticipated. The first such fight between us about Matt and Emma began slowly, silently, but proved to be a force to be reckoned with.

It all started with Matt getting a text from Emma. *Hey... can you get away tonight?*

Now the general unspoken rule was that we did this during the day, during the week. The evenings and weekends were meant for your spouse and family, unless we all got together on a Friday night or something.

Matt showed me the text, and we talked about what this meant and how to handle it.

"I wonder if they got into a fight," I suggested. So far, Matt and I had been able to talk about Steve and Emma's relationship without getting defensive for our extramarital partner.

"Well, Emma mentioned the other day that she's scared Steve's getting suspicious. She said he was being really weird and kind of distant. So maybe they did," Matt offered.

"If Steve's getting weird and suspicious it's because Emma texts you like fifty times a day. I would get suspicious too," I said, immediately flinching by the kitchen sink because I felt myself getting my back up, and I knew Matt heard my tone. I dared look at him while he chopped some potatoes for supper.

He didn't speak, and I knew he was choosing his words carefully. I'd hit a nerve. *Shit.* "But maybe not, maybe she's just feeling guilty," I offered. We'd been at this for a few months now, long enough for it to be categorized as a full-blown affair.

"Maybe I should go meet with her. Maybe she just needs a friend," he said, not looking up.

"Maybe she can call her girlfriends, then. That's what they're there for, Matt," I snapped, putting the bag of rice back in the pantry. "We are not their 'friends,' we're having sex, we're having fun!" I was getting pissed. Even though I knew I'd caused this tension, he wasn't helping.

"Maybe she can, maybe she should," he said, putting the knife down and looking at me. "But she didn't, she called me. And yes, we're in this for fun, but we're not monsters, and we are the cause of this suspicion, so maybe we should step in to fix it before it blows up in our faces." He stood his ground, watching me.

"Fine," I said quietly. "Go. I'll call Steve and see what he's up to, then." Passive aggression is my strong suit.

Matt was quiet for a minute and then he picked up his phone. He texted her back. *I can come after supper. I'll text you when I'm on my way. Let's meet at Sunset's downtown.* Matt read the message to me. "I'll meet her at a bar, no sex, just talking," he said gently.

"Weird that she's texting you and not me about this, don't you think? Maybe you should mention that to her. It will help take the suspiciousness out of everything. Is she stupid?" I threw at him.

He was silent. Inside, I seethed. *Ooh look who can be Mr. Gallant with other women.*

When Matt left, I texted Steve. *I could use a friend right now. You busy?* And I met him at a motel down the street from his place. Fuck *you, Matt. Two can play at this.*

Steve met me within minutes of my arriving. I barely entered the room when I heard him opening the door. There were no "hi, how are you's." I went straight for him and started taking off my shirt. He met me halfway, and we fucked hard and fast.

When Steve and I were done, he shared with me. "I don't know what happened. I feel like all I think about is you, all I want to do is be with you," he started.

Shit. He wasn't getting suspicious of her at all. He was falling for me—and now I'd opened the door to evening trysts. *Thanks, karma, I got it.* And then another thought hit me: Ever had been right. *Son of a bitch.*

"I'm trying to be attracted to Emma, but you're all I want." He kissed me softly on my cheek. "I feel like you're all I've ever wanted." *What the hell?* "I just don't know anymore. Why couldn't I have met you first?" He smiled at some inside joke as his eyes searched mine, hoping for a mirrored response, I supposed.

I leaned in for a hug; I didn't want him to see my face. We lay there for a while, soft kisses, fingers caressing, and the odd nipple twist for good measure. All I could think about lately was the coffee-shop present-time Blake. Steve was a toy, a pawn in a fabulous board game between me and my husband. *Fantastic* in bed; don't get me wrong, but not much more.

"I think it's important to remember that it's fun because we don't have real life to deal with, Steve," I gently began. "This works like this because there aren't bills and cleaning and laundry to get in the way of it. I like it like this. I *like* that we can enjoy all the wonderful things about each of us without all the crap in the way."

"I know. I just feel like we'd be good together too, even with all those things added to the mix." He looked down at our hands. "I feel like I'm falling in love with you."

And that's what it feels like to hit a brick wall going a hundred miles an hour, in case you're curious.

I felt frantic but held it together. I pulled him in and kissed him passionately. I deeply cared for this man. That couldn't be helped. And if I was single, I would totally be into him, into pursuing a relationship. And I told him that. "But that being said," I continued, "I love my husband very much, Steve, and I don't want to promise you something I can't do," I said honestly. I held his face and locked his eyes with mine. "I'm in this for fun … I'm not doing this because Matt is anything less to me … I'm doing this because I want to. I don't know how else to say it. Matt is wonderful to me, to our kids." I pushed away my guilty conscious about my earlier fight with Matt. "He's so good to me. I just want more. Do you know what I mean? It's not him, it's me."

He kissed my hands. "I know," he began. "This is tough. I don't know if I have it in me to keep this up much longer. I love Emma, but you—you're becoming my world. I feel like you're my drug. I need my fix and then I'm okay."

Shit shit shit shit.

"Can I do anything to help? I don't want this to end, Steve. But I need to be honest with you; I'm not leaving Matt," I said as gently as I could.

Fucking stupid male hormones. Stupid Ever for being right. I'm never going to live this down.

"Can we maybe try something different? What do you think would help?" Steve just shrugged. I kissed him and got up. "I have to go. Matt had a showing, and I want to get back before he gets home," I lied—well, half-lied. I *did* want to get back before Matt got home. I wasn't about to share this little get-together with him. "Let's think over the next couple of days, and we'll come up with something, okay?" I quickly got dressed, and without an answer, I left Steve there.

I beat Matt home and ended up quickly showering and watching a *Friends* episode before he got home. He came in and sat beside me. I pretended not to notice.

"Hi … still mad?" he asked. He took off his jacket and threw it on the other couch and waited.

"No. What happened?" I pressed pause on the DVR and turned toward him.

"We had a couple drinks and talked. She told me she's had two other affairs, really short ones—one four months and the other was two weeks. She got caught with the two-week one, so she's paranoid Steve's picking up on something," he explained. "I tried to reassure her it's probably fine; if he'd caught her before and was suspecting that, I was sure he wouldn't hide it. And we talked about cutting the texts down." He played with the bottom of his shirt. "Maybe if Steve is suspicious, it would be the texts, and she agreed."

"Oh, that's good," I said. If only he knew. What was I going to do? Should I tell Matt about Steve falling for me? I thought I should wait it out. Feel how Steve was doing over the next few weeks. If it got any worse, I would tell Matt then. No point getting messy for no reason. Plus, if I told him now, he'd know I was talking to or had been with Steve tonight, and I didn't want to lie. Omission was better for this one.

"Are we okay then?" Matt asked.

I leaned over to him, ready to forgive. "We are, and I'm sorry for freaking out." *Why does he have to be so irritatingly perfect all the time?* I mused. I pressed play so we could finish watching *Friends*.

25

IDIDN'T HEAR FROM STEVE for a few days. It was probably a combination of licking his pride wounds and Emma making every effort to make sure he wasn't thinking she was cheating on him. It was fine by me. I don't like being smothered.

I talked to Ever about Steve's proclamation. Once we got past the *I told you so*'s, we talked about ending this now before it got worse. She told me cheating, no matter the form, never works out. Everyone always thinks they have it under control, she pushed. "I know," I agreed, "but I'm not done with it yet. We'll see what happens," I told her. "If it starts getting worse, I'll pull out." "Hopefully," she said, "before the ground gives out under you guys."

Three days after seeing present-day Blake, he came again. I hadn't missed a morning, waiting for another chance to see him. This time he sat at the table beside mine. I concentrated on breathing in and out. He leaned over after a few minutes and asked if he could steal my business section, if I was done with it. "Sure," was all I could say and fumbled with the pages until I found what he was looking for. He thanked me and took it. *Breathe in…out…*

After a moment, he folded his section and introduced himself. Just like that. I felt twenty again. My skin felt twenty, and my hair, attitude, smile, and that little private part of my heart felt a little warmer. His name was Kaleb. And he was pleased to meet me.

He invited me to join him, and we talked about the coffee shop, where we worked, and the fact that I had a ring on my finger. I excused it away, saying I was free to talk to other human beings even though I'm married. He laughed and agreed with me, to my delight.

Interestingly, he just happened to be in the market for buying a condo; he didn't want to waste any more money renting. Of course, I couldn't have agreed more, so we exchanged business cards.

I sat there for a few minutes after he left, waiting for communication to recommence between my brain and my body. This boy could call himself "Kaleb" all he wanted. He was my Blake reincarnated. He seemed about twenty-four or twenty-five, so I recognize that it was mathematically impossible for him to be Blake, but let's not argue semantics.

The next day I didn't go to the coffee shop. It was so expensive there, I'd spent a small fortune already this past month, and I knew deep down that he wasn't going to be there anyway. He'd met me; there was no reason to go again, unless of course he could afford it and actually went for the coffee. I had fulfilled my destiny. I could get my coffee from my office where we'd invested in one of those fancy single-dose-cup coffee machines with all the flavor cups.

Patience is not one of my strong suits, so after waiting another whole morning, I decided to text him. A friendly reminder that I'm available anytime he wanted to go see some condos. He texted me back that it was a really busy week at work, but maybe Sunday? *Crap.* Sunday meant it wasn't a weekday, and I didn't want to mix anything with my family time. But then again, what was I thinking? This was a man who needed to see condos. This was work.

Sunday would be fine, I told him. I entered his cell into my phone under Kari. Just in case. It was a small addition to that private space in my heart, like a renovation, really. I will probably have a reserved parking spot in hell when I get there.

The mundane activities of real life got in the way the rest of the week. I was irritated, and when poor Steve texted me, I had to force myself to be nice. Kaleb was front and center for the time being, and I wasn't interested in fielding puppy-love texts. But in order to keep up appearances, I would have to, or Matt would get suspicious.

Friday and Saturday night were the worst. Matt suggested going to the club, and I could've even fathom trying to enjoy myself when all I could think about was Sunday. So I suggested a movie date night for us Friday night and a family bowling night with the kids on Saturday. If anyone was going to get me through the next few days, it was going to be my family.

Sunday morning gloriously greeted me, and with a song in my step, the family gathered over a brunch a chef would give me five stars for. I told Matt I had to show some condos to a young girl who was ready to buy a place of her own.

Matt made plans with the kids to nap on the couch, play video games, and eat in the living room. I'd let them race a car through the backyard for all I cared. I told them to enjoy their dog day and got ready. Then I texted Kaleb and told him I'd meet him at Steel's Park, that we'd leave his car there and I'd take him around. He texted back he'd meet me there in an hour.

An hour turned out to be the perfect amount of time. Kaleb was waiting when I got there. He must've spotted me because he was out of his car waiting for me as I pulled up beside him, and he got in.

He looked through the package of listings I'd put together for him, and we discussed the first one on the list. It was a small condo, ground floor, one bedroom, with an open concept. The nice thing, I'd explained to him, was the ground floor condos all have a small garden, big enough for a small patch of grass and room for an intimate patio set and barbecue.

So professional, Leola... try not to rape the poor boy in the bedroom.

When we got there I showed him around, unnecessarily walking behind him (I could just stand in the kitchen and he'd see the whole place on his own). It was tiny but in an incredible location young people flock to. In the bedroom doorway, he stopped. I was inches behind him and talked robotically about the big window facing the central garden of the complex. He turned his head. I breathed him in. Fuck me, he smelled so good his cologne surrounded him like a halo, fingers of it pulling me in closer.

He said, "Yeah, it's pretty nice," and turned back to look in the room.

I stepped back and he turned toward me, brushed past me, and went into the living room to look at the small patio. "I like it," he said. "Let's see some more." And off we went.

The second place was bigger. Still a one-bedroom, but this one had an office space. He walked closer to me, brushing by more, me standing a little bit closer. His eyes were incredible. It felt like I was with Blake again, but he was starting to become all Kaleb, too.

By the third condo, it was all over. I walked behind him into the master bedroom and then into the bathroom ensuite. When he turned to leave the bathroom, I couldn't move.

"You like?" I breathed. My heart was racing, and I was frozen to the spot. He didn't move either, he just stood there looking at me, pondering something. "The bathroom, I mean, of course," I stammered, looking past him. When he didn't answer, I looked back to his face. His eyes were searching mine. He stepped forward and put one arm around my waist and pulled me into him.

"I do," and he crushed my lips to his. I felt my knees give out, and he held me up and took me to the bed. My heart was beating like a hummingbird's, I was afraid for a moment that I would have a heart attack before this could happen. It was a frenzy of clothes, of kissing, of pulling and grabbing. We couldn't get our hands on enough parts of each other. His body was hard, toned, his shoulders wide, his waist narrow—the narrow of a young man who has nothing to do but work out.

I needed to touch *Blake* again. He was harder, more cut where Blake had been softer but I didn't care. I was with the love of my life again. I wanted to crawl inside his body and curl up there forever. He dominated me with eagerness, his big hands holding me to him like we were one. I couldn't even tell you who took off what, it was fast and furious and mad and clawing and wet and hard. Our passion was matched in a heightened dimension. He grabbed me, my hair, crushed my lips, pulled at my hips like the mad intensity of the young in love. My Blake. I was home.

When he kissed me, I felt a chemical reaction. When he entered me, I felt electricity. When it was over, I felt elation. When I left him at his car and he pulled away, I cried and cried and cried.

I felt complete for the first time since Blake's death.

26

I T'S FUNNY. LIFE. I was at work the next morning smiling like a fucking Cheshire cat. I hardly slept the night before; I played everything over and over in my mind till all hours of the night. When his hand pulled me in by the small of my back … what I wouldn't pay to freeze that moment in time, to feel the moment over and over again forever. To bottle it up like an expensive perfume and dab it on my wrists whenever I wanted. And my heart! *Oh* my heart felt ready to burst. My private room was lit; every nook and cranny of that special place was as bright as a Christmas tree. My cheeks hurt from all the smiling I'd done already that morning.

It was how Cassie found me when she came around the corner into my office. "Morning, Leo!" she greeted me this *fine* Monday morning.

"Mornin', darlin," I shot back enthusiastically in my best Southern accent. "What's up?"

"I was checking if Matt was coming in today … it being payday Monday and all," she asked.

Motherfucker. My face fell, and I immediately recovered. "Yes, yes, that's right, he is."

Matt always came in for a few hours around lunch every second Monday as a rule. We usually ordered in Chinese for the three of us and he signed Cassie's paycheck. *Shit, balls.* I wanted today to be mine to live in la-la land.

I pouted like a four-year-old who didn't get the same amount of ice cream as her sister. "Oh good," I lied, "looking forward to some Chinese food!" I forced out some sunshine I had on reserve. Cassie left, and I let my body slump to match my mood.

It turned out to be a great day. It's not often Matt comes in to work, and we always have a fun time on the days he can swing it. We went over some of our listings, had a great lunch, and talked shop. In the moment of the day, I was thankful. I needed a snap back to reality. And I always had the best times with my husband. I loved watching him animated, doing something different than the mundane chores of life, which is when I mostly see him.

At the beginning of lunch, my phone beeped, alerting me of a text. It was Steve. *Hey, beautiful. Hope you're having a great day.*

I told Matt it was a client, and he knew I was lying, but I had to because Cassie was sitting there. During our lunch, which always turns into an informal staff meeting, Steve texted me two more times. *Wanna get together soon?* And twenty minutes later: *Text me when you can! Can't wait to see you again, hottie!!*

Frustration building, I put my phone on silent and went back to Matt and Cassie. Matt's phone, I noticed, had not beeped at all. It looked like Emma heeded his advice on cutting down the texts. *I guess I'm going to have to have the same talk with Steve,* I thought.

After lunch, Cassie left to take care of some showings she had booked. I read Matt the texts from Steve. As he read them, a thought came to mind. "Looks like Steve is getting a bit obsessive, you know?" I planted the seed. "I feel like he's texting me so much. But not like Emma was with texting you. These feel pushy. Persistent." I paused. "Maybe I should talk to him about them like you did with Emma. Maybe it's not malicious intent. Maybe he's just really into this."

"Yeah, I agree. See what he has to say. When are you seeing him again?"

"I don't have any plans yet. I'll text him and suggest tomorrow, I'll get this nipped in the butt sooner than later." Matt agreed.

"Okay, I'm off to show a house on Heritage Hill," I told him. "See you at home. Love you," and I kissed him full on the mouth.

He pulled me close and gave me a wonderful hug. "Love you, too," and he went back to his desk.

I was early meeting my clients at the big Victorian house that I would kill to be able to afford. I texted Steve while I had a minute *Hey there, sorry, busy day. I'm good. Wanna get together tomorrow?*

As I expected, he immediately wrote back. *Yes! Same place 1pm?*

I didn't want to meet so soon, but I had to so I could get a story for Matt on the text messages. This was bordering on a bit too much for my comfort level. This was supposed to be fun.

The next day, I was running late from a phone call so Steve arrived at the hotel before me. He'd only texted me once, saying he was there, asking if I was still coming. I told him I would be there soon.

When I opened the door, he was all casual and I couldn't help but laugh. Poor guy didn't know his ass from a hole in the ground. He was trying so hard.

"Hey there!" I said. He was always a sight for sore eyes. I just needed to curb this behavior before it got bad, but that didn't make me want to stop fucking this hot beast. *Yum.* Like they say, "The only reason I'd throw this one out of bed is to fuck him on the floor." It's one of my favorite sayings. Surprised?

"Hello, beautiful!" He scooped me up in his arms and crushed a kiss on me. The passion was never absent between us, and we wasted no time devouring each other in a mad frenzy.

"I missed you," he said when we were done. "I'm so glad you suggested today. If you hadn't I would've for sure."

"I missed you too," I lied and kissed him full on the mouth.

We talked about what we'd been up to over the last few days. He told me he was trying so hard to pay lots of attention to Emma so she doesn't feel unloved and that they'd had a great weekend together. That he really felt like he'd made great strides making sure she felt important to him and that he was beginning to feel like he could balance this a lot better after our talk.

"Good, that's good!" I praised him.

"I realized," he shared, "that I can be in love with two women. That I *can* do this!" He searched my eyes. *Oh, holy shit.* He kissed me again. "I want to tell you every time I see you, Leola. I love you."

Fuck my life. "I love you too, Steve, but I'm not *in* love with you," I said gently.

"*I'll take it!*" he said. "I'll take it. You have no idea what that means to me."

It means you're an idiot, man. It means I'm trying to be nice. Fucking bloody hell. "I don't want you to think anything is going to change between us, Steve. I'm afraid you're hoping it's going to be something else, and it can't. I have children. I love my husband!" I pleaded for his understanding.

"I know, I know. Don't worry! I'm not expecting anything to happen. I just want you in my life, always. I love you so much. I can't go without you again."

Again? I wondered.

"Okay. Okay." I fought for words as I got out of bed. "Um… I can do this as long as it never changes. Steve, please listen. Matt can never know about us. I'm never going to leave him. I don't want you to make this into something it's not; I just want to be very clear on that, okay?" On my feet at this time, naked, I begged him to get it. Steve got out of bed and came to me. He held my hands in his.

"Leola, I would never tell Matt. I understand you have children and don't want to ruin that for them. But *you* need to understand that I can do this. I can love you both. I *can* give my wife the husband she needs and be your lover. And with all that being said, I need you to understand that I love you." He stopped, kissed my hands, and looked me dead in the eyes. "And I'm *not* going anywhere."

And at that very "safe" moment, in the presence of a man I know loved me, my blood ran cold.

On my way home, I called Ever. There was no answer *again*. I left her a message asking how she was and to please call me back. Was she purposely ignoring me? She couldn't be *that* pissed at me; she usually doesn't put distance between us over difference of opinions. I made a mental note to ask her about it when she called me back.

27

FUNNY THING ABOUT THIS whole Kaleb situation; I had no desire to watch my Cassie's Old Files video. It was weirdly uncomfortable to venture to that part of my brain that separated Kaleb and Blake. In my heart, they shared the same space. The renovation to that room in there was convenient and justified. But in my logical mind, it was like sleeping with two brothers, twins if you will, and—I don't know it was like being caught by your husband while you masturbated. He knows you do it, but it's still weird and you feel guilty when you're caught. It's private, I guess. I just didn't want to cross those with the other on the outside, even though on the inside they were best friends, if not the same person to me.

I called Kaleb Wednesday morning to "see how he liked the condos I'd showed him." He didn't answer, so I left him a professional message. He texted me back that afternoon saying he was out of town on a conference and he'd call me Friday morning. He ended the text with "xoxo," which I took as a good sign. *Friday. Holy shit, that's four hundred years away, for fuck's sake.*

I didn't text him back. I was too pissed.

Thursday was way too long of a day. Steve texted me a few times, but I could tell he was trying to be breezy, so I played with him a bit, even sent him a dirty picture to reward him for his efforts. I didn't hear from him for several minutes. When he did, he just said *thanks for that*, and I told him to delete it before he went home. He said *fine* with a sad–face emoticon and I laughed. He probably downloaded it to his computer.

Thursday night Matt took me out for karaoke with some friends for a birthday, so that was a super fun night and made the time go by faster. I hadn't laughed like that in a while.

And then it was Friday. I took extra time getting ready in the morning, just in case. Kaleb was on the ball and called me on my way to work. My heart leapt when I saw "Kari" come up on the call display. "Good morning," I said, bright and cheery.

"Morning, beautiful girl. Are you busy?" he asked. His voice was enough to make me wet.

"No, I'm just driving to work. How was your conference?"

"Fine. Too long. Over, thank God." He laughed. "Are you busy today? I was wondering if you could show me some places…" he teased.

I tried to concentrate on keeping the vehicle on the road without killing anyone. "I don't have much to do today at all, as a matter a fact. I can make some phone calls when I get to work and get some places on the list, if you'd like," I suggested as casually as I could. Although I just *knew* my voice was reaching too high of a decibel trying to be calm, cool, and collected. Inside I was flying.

"I'd love that." He breathed deeply. "Call me when you can and let me know."

"I will. And Kaleb?"

"Yeah?"

"This time, let's take our time." And I hung up.

I got to work in record time and got the address for one condo that was up for sale and was vacant. The clients left a couch, chair, coffee table, a bed and night stand, and a few decorative touches for viewing purposes. It was a small condo, so less was more, but we wanted people to be able to visualize some furniture in there, because empty it felt really small. So we strategically left a few things here and there to make it look like stuff could fit with room left over. It's a realtor thing. I wasn't planning on showing him any other condos that day, so I didn't need to make any other phone calls.

After texting him the address and the time to meet, I left work and got there ten minutes early to make sure he didn't have to wait in unfamiliar surroundings. I left the door to the apartment open a few inches so he could just come in.

He arrived right on time and looked better than the last time. A smile spread on his face when he walked in and closed the door.

My legs thankfully remembered to work, and I got up off the couch to approach him. I slowly walked over, and he put his hands out and took mine. "Hi," was all he said and I didn't answer.

Kaleb looked down at me, and I smiled shyly and looked down. He let go of my hands and brought my chin up so I could look in his eyes again.

And then he kissed me. Blake's love filled my whole body as I kissed Kaleb back. My arms went around his neck and his went around my waist, and he kissed me with everything he had. When I pulled away, my face went immediately into his neck, and his arms caressed my back, and he held me with everything he had.

"I missed you," he said, and I blinked back tears of love and confusion and logic.

We walked into the bedroom, Kaleb walking backward, guiding me in with his mouth. I pulled at my shirt, and he took his off and then he reached behind and unhooked my bra. His hands were firm on my back, and he held me like we were long-lost lovers who didn't want to break the spell. He kissed me deeply, softly, firmly, drinking me in. My heart felt like it would burst with the love I felt. I told myself that he wanted me, he missed me, he loved me. This was my fantasy.

He lowered me to the bed, and without missing a beat or separating our bodies, he entered me gently, filling me with his hard cock. He stroked himself in my wet pussy, slowly feeling every inch of each other, memorizing everything. I lay there, feeling the weight of him on me, and my arms went around his shoulders. I was lost in him. His arms were around me, my legs wrapped around his waist as I clung to him. I kissed his face, his mouth, his nose, his cheeks, his eyes. Every part of him belonged to me, every part of him I've missed over these last twenty years. I had to make up for lost time.

He filled me deeply, each time taking it out to the very tip, only to push it back in so we could feel the whole length of each other over and over and over. He kissed me fully, partly, nibbling my bottom lip, sucking on my tongue, his breath falling over me like a blanket. My heart was swollen ten times too big for my chest. I couldn't breathe deep enough to fill my lungs. I wanted our bodies to become one so he would never leave me again. We finally came together, hard and fast. We clung to each other, not wanting to miss a single shiver, a single heartbeat, a single breath we'd shared, our bodies willed to become one. He'd made love to me like we were Romeo and Juliet in a forbidden love.

Of course, Kaleb didn't know how deep my feelings were for him, this boy I barely knew. But I could feel his feelings, could feel them as much as mine.

When we were done, we lay quietly for a long time, not moving. How did he know this was what I needed? Then slowly, not moving from where we'd fallen, we talked, sharing everything about each other as if we had to catch up on what we'd missed all these years, which is exactly what I was doing.

Kaleb's father left his mother when she was six months' pregnant with him. His father had lost his father to suicide shortly after the Vietnam War. He just couldn't handle life anymore. Kaleb's father had been twelve when his father took his life. When Thomas met Kaleb's mother, Sandy, they were seventeen years old and so in love. They were together only four months when she got pregnant, but it proved to be too much for Thomas, and he accused her of cheating and said the baby wasn't his and he left. Sandy found out thirteen years later that Thomas was homeless and living somewhere in New York.

Kaleb only had a handful of photos his mother had kept

for him. She never remarried, and Kaleb was an only child. He bought a duplex with his mom and they lived side by side for now, having their own space, but he was there to mow the lawn and shovel in the winter and could be there for her in an emergency. He told me it was a great arrangement. His mom was the best, and she was busy with her work and her friends and was a great friend to him. So you really *don't* need a condo, I'd chided him. He laughed.

I shared my story. I did not share Blake, nor did I share Steve and Emma. I did tell him, however, that I had cheated on my husband before with Lori, which is the truth, and that I love my husband very much and that I didn't know what it was about him that I couldn't resist, which is a bald-faced lie, but that I wouldn't mind doing this again sometime, if he was up for it. He leaned over, brushed his hair out of his eyes—*kill me*—and kissed me. And then he told me he would do it every day if he could. Exactly *not* the right thing to tell me, I ruefully thought. But I took it as a good sign.

28

BY THE TIME I got back to my car, I had two missed calls and seven text messages. Both missed calls were from Steve. Five of the seven text messages were also from Steve. The other two were from Matt saying, *One of these days traffic is going to kill me, haha,* and the other said, *Love you, hope you're having a good day.* The five messages from Steve were odd. He'd never texted me so many times in one day before; never mind in the span of two hours.

Hi, beautiful.

Whatcha doing?

Leola? Text me when you can. I miss you.

Must be having a busy day. Hope you're doing well.

You there? What are you doing?

The phone calls were both just hang-ups. Finding this odd, I texted Steve back right away. *Hey, Steve. Sorry, got hung up. What's up?*

On the drive back to work, I called Matt. While I was calling him, Steve texted me back, but I ignored it.

Matt answered on the second ring. "Hey, babe!"

"Hi there! You sound a lot happier than your traffic text. How's your day?" I sang lightly, the guilt successfully punched down as far as I could.

He laughed. "I know, right? I was ready to road rage someone's ass earlier. My day is better now. Busy, but better, how about you?"

"Mine's good," I said. "Busy. What do you want to do this weekend?" I wanted to change the subject as quickly as possible. I was looking forward to some family time. "Do you want to take the kids swimming or something?"

"Sure, let's hit the beach for sure; it's supposed to be a beautiful weekend."

"That sounds perfect. Let's barbecue at home and have some friends over for a fire in the backyard. Maybe some hot tub later or something," I suggested.

"That sounds perfect. Do you want to do the club tonight? We haven't all been together for a while, the four of us. I think we should; we need to keep up appearances."

I paused. He was right, but Steve was being weird. "Sure, that sounds really good," I lied. *Ugh.* "I'll send Emma a text when I get back to work."

At a red light I quickly checked Steve's text. *Where've u been? I was worried.* I rolled my eyes. When I got back to work I sent Emma a text about going out tonight. She texted me back a while later, saying she talked to Steve and they were in. *Fucking super.* I texted Steve back and told him I was showing a house to clients and that I would see him tonight.

And I called Ever. Again. She *still* hadn't gotten back to me from the other day.

She answered as if nothing was wrong. "Hey!" she said cheerfully.

"*Hey?*" I shot back. "What's going on? Are you okay? I haven't heard from you."

"Sorry, hon. Been busy. What's up?"

"Well nothing much, I guess. Just missing you. I was worried. I don't think we've ever gone this long without talking."

"I know. No, it's all good. What are you guys up to this weekend?"

It felt like she was changing the subject. "Well, we're going to the club tonight and then thought about maybe a barbecue Saturday night. Can you guys come?"

"Sure, we have no plans."

"Okay, come over whenever, then," I said. "I'll be out grabbing stuff for supper and should be home anytime after four."

"Okay, hon. See you tomorrow. Love you!"

The kids had no plans that night, so I rented a movie and got them all snuggled down with popcorn and soda with the instructions for bedtime. I never worried about them together. Charlie was so protective of Heather. When she was a little girl, she broke her arm on the trampoline, and he slept beside her at the hospital and read her stories at home for the whole first day. He was wonderful with her. He was just like his dad, who had taught him well.

I gave them big hugs and kisses and closed the blinds and locked the doors. While I did that, we talked about the fun day we were going to have the next day.

On the way to the club, we talked about how lucky we were to have them in our lives. How so many people struggle to have kids, or who have them and there's either medical trauma they have to live through, disabilities, or parents who lose their children. We were so lucky, and we really tried to remember that all the time.

When we got to the club, it was half-full. Steve and Emma were already there at our usual table, and they greeted us with big smiles and hugs and kisses. Steve held me tighter than usual, and I thought about telling Matt soon about this newfound clinginess. I thought about trying to talk briefly to Steve tonight about watching it or Emma would find out.

As the night progressed, I watched Matt and Emma together when I could, and it occurred to me I'd lost touch about where their relationship had led to. Other than the one small fight Matt and I'd had about Emma calling him and Matt's and my "Shag 'n Brag" sessions, their relationship was either plain-Jane good or they were just not that into each other. There didn't seem to be the passion Steve and I shared. And as I watched them through the night, they were casual and friendly and easygoing. I was jealous of the ease they seemed to have with each other. I felt as if Steve and I were heading toward disaster. I needed to talk to Matt.

When Steve asked me to dance, I accepted and kissed Matt on the way to the dance floor. Steve held me close, and we danced quietly for a moment. I was distracted all night, and dancing with him didn't change that.

It was Steve who started. "I missed you today," he said. When I didn't answer right away, he added, "I don't like it when you don't answer me."

Taken aback, it took me a moment to answer. "I was working, Steve—and besides, what if I was with Matt? Sometimes I can't answer you right away," I explained as calmly as I could.

"You can just say it's a client and answer the phone. If you say hello and make up some name and say you're busy and that you'll call me back, at least I'd know you're not ignoring me. You know what I mean? I told you I loved you. That means something to me, you know," he finished.

The earth's gravitational pull seemed stronger. "I realize that, Steve. But you have to understand that I cannot be available all the time. Even my kids know that." My voice got thicker, like wading through gravy. Purposeful.

Steve didn't answer right away. Then he kissed my cheek. "I get it," and he forced a smile. He pulled away as soon as the song ended and went back to our table. I had exactly two seconds to compose myself and join our group. Emma and Matt were on their feet at the table, and when I joined Matt, he pulled me in and we stood like that talking with Steve and Emma for a little while, like nothing was wrong.

I stole glances at Steve, and he was animated, but I could tell he was covering a darkness. It was time for Matt and me to talk about where this was going and how long it was going to go on. Matt and Emma were too good of friends. Steve was making me nervous.

This social experiment was approaching its expiration date.

29

THANKFULLY, STEVE KEPT TO himself for the rest of the weekend. Perhaps he'd gotten his fill the night before.

Saturday turned out to be a really great day with the kids, and Saturday night we had a few friends over and roasted marshmallows over the fire pit, and Charlie played his guitar and we sang around the fire. It was a great night.

Ever and Clint hadn't arrived until around seven. I privately took her aside and said, "What the fuck? I said I'd be home at four!"

She said she got hung up *but was there now, so fuck off!* And she laughed and "cheered" my drink.

I was worried Matt and my lifestyle choice of late was maybe bothering her more than she was willing to admit. But that didn't seem to be it. It wasn't like her.

On Sunday, the kids went to their friends' houses to hang out, so Matt and I had some time alone. I talked to him about Steve and his increasing interest in me. I told him about the texts, the conversation on Friday night, and the general uneasiness I'd been feeling. And of course, I had to tell him about Steve being in love with me.

"What should we do, babe?" I asked him. "Fuck me; I didn't want it to come to this."

Matt was taking this all in stride, really thinking about every option we had and what our angles might be. "Well, I think maybe we should end this before it all goes to shit, right? We always said this was going to be fun, and it doesn't sound like you're having much fun."

"I *am* having fun. I just didn't want love to be part of it. I don't know why he has to do this—everything was perfect for all of us," I complained. Fucking piece of shit, that Steve. He was my distraction for Matt so I could be with Kaleb. Aargh!

"Yes it was. But now not so much." Matt paused for thought. "I think the best way to do it is slowly, over the next week or so; we need to wean ourselves off. Wait—*I know*!" He snapped his fingers. "The easiest way to do it is tell them our spouses are getting suspicious. Tell him I found a text and was questioning you and that you had to make a lie to get out of it and now it's just all too stressful. And I'll do the same with Emma!"

"Aw, babe you're a genius! That's perfect! Okay, then. Done!" I smiled and wrapped my arms around his neck and gave him a big smooch.

When I got to work Monday morning, Cassie was already there and on the phone when I walked in. She asked the caller to hold and said there were flowers for me in my office and commented on how wonderful my husband was. I stuck my tongue out at her and walked into the back.

Cassie had placed my orange and blue flowers by the window. I bent over to smell them and looked for a card but there wasn't one. It didn't matter; a silent, humble "I love you" from Matt is better than any stupid card. I sent him a quick "thank you and I love you" text and set about my work.

A few minutes later when I read the return text, I frowned as I read two question marks from Matt. And then I realized he hadn't sent them. One quiet moment I thought maybe Kaleb, but he was too young for that kind of flattery. It was then that I realized they were most likely from Steve. I took a deep breath and looked at the flowers on the windowsill. *Shit.*

It was only an hour later when Steve called and asked if I'd received anything special at work today. Instead of playing dumb I thanked him and asked him if he was busy the next day to meet. He said he could swing it, and we set up a time at our usual spot.

It was weird to think how far Matt and I had come with this whole thing. We had talked about every angle, we were respectful of each other, and I was sad to think this was going to end. I loved how we balanced our lives. It felt like we lived in a magical world. I had my very own magic wand and could ask for anything. I guess I'd used up my three magic wishes and was left with an empty feeling now. Fuckin' Steve. What a piece of shit, fucking this all up! Emma kept Matt distracted so I could have what I have, whatever it was, with Kaleb. Fucking bloody hell. I felt like kicking Steve's ass.

When Steve came into the hotel room, I went straight to him. I was so sad that this was going to end. I wasn't crying or anything, but I made a purposeful effort to remember everything, to remember every line, every crevice this last time together. He held me tight and kissed me hard. We wasted no time getting to it. And it just kept fucking getting better, damn him!

I wanted to take my time, but I had to be careful to not confuse him with making love. That would only make things worse. I just enjoyed it and let it flow naturally, just with the heightened awareness to remember everything I could.

When we were done, we lay there together for a while. It took me some time to get up the nerve to start the dreaded conversation. "Steve, I have some bad news," I began as I'd practiced on the drive over.

"Nothing can be that bad," he said, kissing my hand.

"Well… it kind of is. Matt found a text from you over the weekend that I forgot to delete, and I had to lie my way out of it." Steve froze. "I don't know if he bought it, but I feel just awful now and don't know if it's such a good idea that we keep this up,"

I said in one breath. I dared look at him. His face was sad and mad. There was no movement, no sound from either of us for a few minutes. It felt like forever.

"I can't let you go, Leola," he said simply. It was not a plead, it was a statement. "I don't know what I'd do without you."

"I know!" I played with it. "I feel the same way, but, Steve, I can't let this affect my marriage, my kids." I pulled all the ace cards.

"Well," he started slowly, "maybe you should've thought about that before we started this." It was barely audible.

My insides turned to ice. I couldn't move. I couldn't breathe. My heart stopped beating. "You're probably right," I said lightly. "But I didn't and here we are … I have loved everything, Steve, and I don't want this to end," I pleaded truthfully, "but I just can't risk it. I'm so sorry. I don't know what else to do. I don't want Matt to find out, I don't want my kids to find out, I don't want him to tell Emma, I don't want your marriage to end." I begged him to see every angle.

Steve got out of bed and got dressed. He came over and kissed me. "Everything will be fine. I promise," he said between kisses. "Don't worry, Leola. It'll all be right, okay? I'll make everything okay again."

And then he left me there. And I truly had no idea if it had gone well… or bad.

I got my things together and stepped out into the hall. As always, I checked both ways just in case. No one was down to the left, and looking to the right I saw a man I didn't recognize come out of his room. Feeling safe, I walked into the hall and let the hotel room door close. The man smiled at me as he walked past, and as I approached the room he'd just exited, the door opened again and out walked a woman.

She turned to look at me before going the opposite way.

Unfortunately, our eyes caught.

Ever.

I froze on the spot, like gravity had just upped itself tenfold. My feet anchored where they were. My eyes bugged out like someone was holding a gun to my head. Neither of us spoke for what felt like forever. Ever's eyes darted down the hall, seemingly trying to calculate if her lover was far enough away that I didn't see him come out of this very same room as her. I turned to look and saw his back just rounding the corner to the elevators and looked back at her.

"Hey," I started.

She exhaled, long and deep, the air she'd been holding. Her eyes closed and she looked down. "Hey," she parroted.

"I don't know what to say," I said awkwardly.

She didn't respond. We stood there, neither of us knowing what to do. I looked at her as she played with her purse.

"Can we go in your room and talk?"

She looked at the door with desperation. I was sure she was contemplating what it looked like in there.

"I know what went on; it's not like the state of the room is going to shock me now," I pressed.

She reluctantly turned around, fished the key card out of her purse, and opened the door. I followed her inside and asked if she happened to have any hard liquor. She laughed and said unfortunately no. Ever went to the bed and moved the covers over, climbed in, and sat cross-legged in the middle. I sat down at the little table and put my purse down.

We sat quietly for a moment. I looked at the floor and in my peripheral vision saw her playing with the blankets.

"So," I began and shrugged. "What's going on, babe?" She sat like a teenager who got caught smoking. "How long?"

It took her a moment, but she gathered her pride and looked at me. "A while, I guess. I don't know what to say, Lee," she pleaded.

"Me neither. I don't understand. After all the chastising you've given me over the last couple months—you've been doing this the whole time?"

"I know. I guess I was worried you'd see right through me. I'm so sorry."

"Is this something Clint knows about? Who is he?"

"No, Clint doesn't know. He would kill him. His name is Paul, and he's a nurse at the hospital." She paused. "We've been flirting for like five years. It came to a head a few months ago." She shook her head. "I don't plan on it going on for very long. I just needed to feel *it* again, you know?" I nodded. "But now I feel like I'm falling for him. I feel like he's—oh my God, I don't know what the fuck to do."

She surrendered her feelings to me, to herself. She slumped on the bed like her backbones had been stripped from her like a fish. "We've been such great friends at work for so long; we spent so much time together, all these years. It's so hard." She was baring her soul. The tough Ever I knew sat somewhere in the shadows. This Ever was raw and scared and exposed. "I don't want to lose my husband, Lee! Please don't tell him! I just want to get through this so Clint and I can be good again. So I can be good for him again."

I sat silently for a while. Ever wiped away her tears. They were tears of frustration, of being pissed off for being caught, of letting her guard down. The tough exterior was a little transparent, and I knew that was the worst part of this for her.

"I hear you, babe. I really do. You know, it's funny." I let out a quiet laugh. "If you were a guy friend doing this to his wife, I would threaten him that he has to stop or I would tell my girlfriend. If you were a guy and you were Matt's friend, and you guys were doing the whole *guy code* fucking bullshit thing, I would lose my shit." I stopped. "But I'm sitting here and I... *fuck me, Ever*—I have no idea what to do. Because I *hear* what you're saying." I stopped. I was incredulous with myself. I had *no fucking idea* what to say to her to make this better. To make it stop for her. To make it right. "Did you go to New York with him?"

"Yes," she whispered. "I'm sorry I lied to you, Leola." She looked at me desperately.

"I know," I said quietly. "Okay, well, I have to go. Let's talk about this soon, okay?" I looked at her and she nodded and looked at her lap. "And is it fair to say you need to come up with some kind of plan? You can't live like this, right?"

"Okay," she said.

And we got up and I went to her and helped her off the bed and we embraced. I gave her a kiss and said we'd talk soon and I left her there.

With a heavy heart, I walked out.

30

THERE HE WAS, STANDING by the car waiting for me. Not looking at anything, but you could tell he was taking it all in. Refueling his soul with the smells and the sounds of nature, he loved the outdoors, loved the wind, the sun, the smells. Life. He loved life and everything that came with it.

I walked back to where we'd pulled over on this almost-deserted highway, from where I'd hidden myself in the bushes to pee, and as I watched him, I'd fallen in love with him all over again. He was mine. I felt an almost primal rush of feelings, clashing between wanting to devour him like I'd stumbled upon the greatest animal that would feed and clothe my family for a month and a maternal love of protection and ownership. It was a mad game of tennis, back and forth, back and forth.

Sometimes it felt like a struggle to settle somewhere in the middle to where he was safe from harm and safe from smothering by me. Either way it was the innocent and passionate love of the young. Remember that? Remember not being afraid of being hurt, of death, or of the future? Remember when we felt invincible…?

When Blake noticed I was back, he flashed a wide smile of white teeth. "I was getting worried there. Thought a bear might've stolen you away from me!" He grabbed me about the waist and I laughed as he kissed my neck.

"I think a bear's hug would've been less painful than this!" I gasped, laughing, struggling to get away.

He chased me around the car, and I beat him to my passenger door, clamored in, and locked it as quickly as I could. I stuck out my tongue and laughed as he pouted and stomped back to his side, a crooked smile sneaking out of the corner of his mouth.

When he reached for the door handle, I saw the driver's side door start to fall away, like sand falling through fingers. I reached over to grab the handle and saw Blake pounding on the window, calling for me. I yelled back for him to help me, but his seat and the steering wheel began to fall away too. I scrambled back to my side of the car, grasping for anything to hold on to. I looked over at Blake, and all I saw was what was left of his body disintegrating into sand, falling into nothingness, his face showing no emotion, just watching me as I screamed in terror.

I woke with a start, my eyes bugging out of my head as I tried to remember how to breathe. My room was dark, and it took me a moment to realize it was still night. I looked at the clock: 3:38. Moving as slowly as I could to not disturb Matt, I got out of bed, grabbed my housecoat to cover my naked body, and silently left the room.

In the living room, still in the dark, I sat on the couch and hugged my knees. There were no tears; I only felt a sense of dread. Which was weird—usually I felt deep sorrow mixed with comfort when I dreamed of Blake. But this time it was more a feeling of fear. It unsettled me, sitting alone in the dark. It felt like eyes were watching me, like something was waiting for me. My thoughts switched to Steve and Ever, and my mind went to the last few months.

Clearly this was an anxiety-induced dream, which didn't take a rocket scientist to figure out. And as I looked through my living room bathed in moonlight, it occurred to me my sense of security was still there. I could still do this, I told myself firmly. Steve wasn't running this fucking show! Anger built in the pit of my stomach. *Fuck him! He thinks he's going to ruin what I have here? No fucking way.* Kaleb was my heart and soul right now.

I *needed* him. No matter what happened with Steve and Emma, in our lives or not, nothing was going to take this away from me. Nothing and no*body.*

Feeling the strength building in me, I focused on Matt and me. *We* were running this fucking show. This was *my* idea. *Fuck you,* Steve! I couldn't believe I'd let him even *try* to weasel himself into some pathetic soft spot in my heart. Matt and I had set this whole thing up, we'd completed our mission; our social experiment had been successful. We'd controlled every aspect of these last few months. If Steve thought he was going to play some sort of bullshit game with *me,* he had another think coming. *Go fuck yourself, Steve.*

Leola's back in the game now...

31

*C*HOICE: AN ACT OR *instance of choosing; selection; the right, power, or opportunity to choose; option; an abundance or variety from which to choose.*

Here's the funny thing about life. It's all about choices. Or the lack thereof.

I didn't have a choice when Blake was taken from my life. I had choices when it came to the way I dealt with it. Or did it? I guess on some level, looking back, yes. But as anyone knows, sometimes you're just on autopilot and your body performs the automatic functions of just staying alive.

How much of life is about preparedness and how much is reactive? How much is fate? How much of it is Karma? There are so many rudimentary factors it is impossible to calculate: Emotions; primal instincts; learned behaviors; anger; love; fear; jealousy; past memories.

Too many variables. The list is endless. Who is one person to judge how anyone should react? There are primal reactions to many things, but there are also the parents whose children die, and they can react from one end of the spectrum to the other, from screaming to silence. But judge we must. There is always a hierarchy. It is in us all. Even animals have a social class within their own species, not to mention the food chain. There is always an alpha male.

Or female.

And choose we must. Ever is making her own choices. Am I to be the alpha female here and let her stand before me to plead her case? We all make choices that are totally justified to suit our individual needs. Does that make her right or wrong? Who says? Are Matt and I "more right" than Ever because we are not lying to each other where Steve and Emma are concerned? After all, we're forcing them to lie to each other to suit our needs.

Matt and I have made a lot of choices throughout this journey. Unfortunately, I gave Steve some rope, played with him a little, but almost got myself hung at the gallows with it. Give someone an inch and they take a mile … stupid clichés. Now I'm faced with another choice. Do I rein the rope in, pile it nicely beside the shed—or do I take him to the gallows?

What are his crimes, really? Let's weigh the options. He got caught up in our game, he felt too much, panicked a little when he felt his world turning … is that reason enough to hang him with it? He did some good, too. He made me feel great about myself through his compliments, flowers, and attention. Wicked lover. Kept up his part of the "secret" from his wife and from my husband, which is normally important. All in all, he's batting a good game. A couple of fouls, but that's to be expected, right? Maybe I should cut him a little slack…

Fuck that.

Playing a little game of "fuck me behind your wife's back" is as old as time. Steve was crossing some major lines with me, not to mention making the hair stand up on the back of my neck. And having a second chance at repairing my broken soul from Blake's death with Kaleb was… I can't even begin to articulate what that meant to me. Imagine having that one person in your life taken from you and then given a second chance to be with him, to feel that part of you whole again. To fill that void, that emptiness that never *ever* goes away was worth more to me than anything. I had a chance to be complete again. My family, my children were nothing short of perfection and brought me as close to complete as I could possibly get. Blake's unexpected death at such a vulnerable time in my life- that almost-adult,

I'm-figuring-out-who-I-am time in your life- stalled part of me at that age. I felt I was holding hands with that part of me, that young Leola that got left behind, pulling her along—*catch up, come join me now.*

I couldn't bear to think, *What would happen if I let go of her now...?*

32

MATT'S SHAG 'N BRAG session for his last time with Emma was bittersweet. By the time he was done recounting their afternoon together, I was ready to fuck his brains out; I was so wet knowing this was the last story.

I thought as he was telling me, *Perhaps I could run into Emma sometime on my own...* and as I thought that, I couldn't believe I didn't think of it sooner. Disappointment washed through me, reaching every inch of my body and diluting desire like smoke filling a room with the deepest exhale. I touched myself as I listened to Matt describe each detail. I played with his cock as he twisted my nipples, and I tried to keep the moaning down to a minimum to not interrupt him.

Tasting myself and then rubbing my juices on the head of his hard-on, I was dying to push his face between my legs but didn't want him to stop telling this last story, dripping with picturesque commentary of Emma's naked body writhing against him. Instead, I wet my fingers between my legs again and continued the silky massage of the head of his cock.

He inhaled and held it for a moment. I panicked a bit because he stopped talking, and I didn't want him to stop. To never stop. But it was too late. I played with him a bit, and his mouth found my nipple, sucking hard. I fought as long as I could until I could stand it no more. My hands went to his head, tangling my fingers in his soft locks, pushing his face into my breasts, squeezing and begging him to suck harder.

His fingers entered me and I clung to him, my long legs wrapping around his back with my head flung back on the bed. *Suck harder. Harder,* I begged.

One hand held me tight, and I bucked as his other hand worked hard against my pussy. I wanted him inside me. I pulled his head off my breast, the suction so strong I cried out in desire and pain. His mouth crushed mine and we kissed and sucked on lips and tongues. His body moved over mine and he entered me with force, holding my arms above my head. He fucked me hard, pumping madly. When I squirmed to get free he held me tighter, firming his grip on my wrists. He watched me as I struggled, my hips moving him deeper with every thrust.

His hand moved to briefly close around my neck and I stopped; he stilled his hand there for a moment and then caressed me gently there until he reluctantly and slowly moved around to the back of my neck. We were still for a moment and locked eyes. He let go of me then, and I waited for only a second and then grabbed him, wrapped one leg around him, and flipped him over on the bed, not missing a beat as I rode him from above.

Deeper now I crushed against him, grinding my clit, rubbing the head of his cock deep inside me, my momentum increasing with every thrust. His fingers dug into my ass as he guided me faster and faster, my hands clawing at his shoulders. I couldn't hold back anymore—it was too much. I leaned back for his cock to rub my G-spot. When I grabbed at his thighs behind me, holding him hard, he let go of me to grasp at the sheets. I thrashed violently, rubbing my G-spot with the head of his cock; I felt the warmth escalating until I couldn't take any more.

Release was all there was left and I came hard, crying out, and he grabbed me again, pushing me down harder, and he cried out as we came together. I felt him pumping warmth into me as I pushed hard on him, furiously rubbing against him as I came and came and came. He held me down to him as I bucked; it was so slippery as I squirted all over, my juices running down between his legs, onto his hips and stomach. I pressed my weight against him, not ready for my orgasm to end, and I slowed my rhythm as his grip on me loosened. We stayed in our own worlds for a moment as my hips rubbed against him slowly, and I leaned toward him. His arms went around me and we fell together exhausted, sweating and breathing hard.

We did not move for a few minutes, just lay where we fell until we could regain the ability to breathe again and let the blood drain back to where it should be, to a regular beat. Slowly I started to move and heaved myself to a comfortable position beside him, a permanent smile planted on both our faces; we looked at each other and laughed.

"Sorry you didn't get to finish your story," I whispered.

"Story? What story?" Matt laughed. "There is no story that could even begin to warrant an apology after *that.*" He gestured at the two of us. "*Never* say sorry for that, babe." He leaned over for a sweaty kiss.

I laughed and I leaned forward to meet his kiss. "Well, I'm pretty sad to see those Shag 'n Brag sessions go," I said with a pout. "Maybe we can do that with someone else once a year or something."

Matt lay on his back and looked at the ceiling. "Yes, most definitely," he agreed. There was a moment of comfortable silence as we digested the fact that this was all over.

"Do you feel like any part of you fell in love with Steve, Leola?" Matt's voice was barely audible. He didn't look at me.

I turned to look at him, but when he didn't move I propped myself up on my arm and addressed him firmly. "Not one bit," I said honestly. When he still didn't move I gently continued. "I don't know. It never became about that for me, I guess. When Steve told me he was in love with me and I had to explain to him why it was all sunshine and roses, my answer seemed to come out of nowhere but from a place of understanding and honesty. Remember? I told him it's all great because there are no bills to pay and kids' shitty asses to wipe and stuff like that. It wasn't real. And I truly felt that. It wasn't even something I had to think about; it just came out."

I reached for Matt's hand, and he finally turned to me. "*You* are the only one I'm in love with," I said, pushing Kaleb out of my mind. I meant it, though. I realized then that Kaleb wasn't someone I was *in love* with and wanted to share my life with. He was my personal portal to my former self.

And I think he was here to help me finally put that part of my life away. The way it should have been put away in the first place.

Matt smiled and squeezed my hand. "Good" was all he said. I asked him the same question back. "There were a few times where I felt like we were playing with fire," he admitted.

My heart skipped a beat. "What stopped you?" I asked quietly. I thought again how I was so distracted by Kaleb and by Steve's persistence that Emma and Matt were pretty much on their own with this, not a lot of accountability. It hadn't dawned on me through this whole process how selfish I'd been, how close I could've been to losing my marriage.

"I think maybe because we had so many rules and were both part of the whole process; it was more of a job, a mission if you will, that those kinds of feelings stayed far enough away. It wasn't private, I guess. Maybe that's why Steve fell for you. It was all his, and he could do with it was he wanted. I don't know if Emma feels like she's falling in love with me, though. If she does, she hasn't said anything. Maybe because she still feels guilty about her other affairs, so she didn't let herself fall for me? I don't know. It's all too much, you know?" He played with our intertwined fingers as he spoke.

Part of me felt relief. Part of me felt maybe he was trying to convince himself as much as me. And that part of me hoped he was so I would feel less guilty about Kaleb. I briefly thought about Ever. Oh the tangled webs we weave.

"I love you, Matt." I breathed quietly and kissed his shoulder. We lay there for a moment in silence and Matt drew me into his arms and took a deep breath. I wanted to crawl inside him, and for a moment I was perversely jealous that he could physically enter me, truly and literally feel me from the inside. I wanted to do the same and tuck away inside him where it is dark and warm and safe. Sometimes it is all too much. And as much as I wanted to do as I pleased and as much as I had control over every part of my life, there were times I just yearned for a simpler time where the "perfect life" existed. But the realization inevitably came as it always did, and I succumbed to the fact that their grass was no greener than I'd imagined. And again my thoughts drifted to Ever.

Life is interesting. As much as you think *they*'ve got it all figured out and put together, you just never really know. The realization that no one is better at any of this than I am was a confidence booster.

33

I KNEW I WAS GOING to have a hard time with Ever's situation as I came to realize, much to my dismay, that it was a direct reflection on me and my choices with Kaleb. *For fuck's sake.* Not wanting to confront those issues, I kept Ever at a distance for a few days. I didn't want to have to talk about anything that had to make me internally defend my relationship with Kaleb. That was justified and no one could possibly understand what I was going through and how much I needed this to get through the next twenty years of my life. I don't know what I would do if it was taken away from me. Hypocritical or not, I couldn't stand in judgment of Ever.

It is amazing what graces we give others when it stands to defend our own interests. I could never be a real courtroom judge.

Not surprisingly, I didn't hear from her for a few days either, but when I did, my heart soared. She sent me only a little text: *Hey, babe... go fuck yourself??* I smiled as I read it.

I wrote her back: *Only if you're there with me.*

And then my phone rang. "Hey, babe," I answered, and a small smile of contentment appeared on my face. "How are you?"

"I'm okay," she answered quietly. "I miss you so much. I don't know what to do."

"Me neither. And I can't tell you what to do. This is your life, and I just hope you know what you are doing." I sat on the couch on this sunny but windy Friday morning and hugged my knees. "I'll love you through it, okay?"

"Yeah." She sighed.

"It is so crazy. Life. I still feel like I'm twenty years old, you know?" I pointed out honestly. Fuck how I wanted to tell her about Kaleb. So we could wade through this muddy swamp together. I wanted to tell her so badly and knew it would make her *and* me feel better, but the other half of me just wanted to keep it all to myself. I didn't want to talk about it. To anyone. It would be like talking to your friend about your counseling session. It's private—the breakthroughs you make with a counselor were something you didn't want to expose to anyone. And it was still a gaping wound for me, so adding anything or anyone to it would be like rubbing salt in. It would sting beyond even the highest pain threshold.

"I think I'm just going to trust you with it, Ever. I have so much going on with this whole Steve and Emma thing, and it's not that you're not important, I just don't want to muddy the waters any more than I need to. I'm here if you need me, but I think I should clean out my own backyard before I start raking yours. Is that cool?"

"Yes! Yes, that's totally cool. What's going on?" She pried, eager for the spotlight to be off her. I told her what was going on, how Steve was getting weird, his proclamation to me, and how Matt and I were taking back control.

"Holy shit!" she cried. "That's fuckin' intense. Do you know what you're going to do?"

"Not quite yet. I have some ideas, but I think I'm going to have to be on my toes for this one. He seems to know what he's doing."

"Okay, let me know if there's anything I can do for you. I gotta run." She paused. "I love you, Leola."

"I love you more," I said and hung up.

I sat on the couch for a minute and shook my head in amazement. *I'm gonna have to clean up a lot of shit before Dr.*

Phil comes knocking on my door for my so-called revolutionary marriage advice. Fuck. Fuckin' bloody hell.

And then the doorbell rang. I got off the couch, totally pissed that my morning was going to be interrupted by some unwanted call. I had a sign on my mailbox specifically stating No Soliciting. They were such a pain in the ass to get rid of, and I quickly wished Ever was here to tell them to fuck off. I opened the door, and when I saw who was standing there, I froze.

Kaleb.

My body was cemented in place. What the fuck was he doing here, and how did he know where I lived? He looked at me with worry, and as my blood started to flow again, I quickly invited him inside. "What the hell are you doing here?" I scolded him like a ten-year-old child. "My husband could've been home! My kids could've been off school today, Kaleb! What were you thinking?"

"I'm so sorry," he said over and over as I guided him down the hall to the kitchen.

"Well, what the fuck?" I demanded. *God, he's so fucking hot.* I couldn't believe he was in my kitchen. I went to him and hugged him and kissed him deeply, and as I pulled away I noticed the look on his face. This was not a lover's afternoon-delight call. "What?" I asked, more concerned now.

"I'm so sorry," he repeated. He was nervous, but he was also pissed. He looked pointedly at me. "Tell me who Steve is and why he's calling me."

34

HINDSIGHT IS 20/20. *FUCK me,* another cliché. I *hate* when shit like that is *so* true—but not only true, but the fact it's been ignored or not given the proper amount of emphasis is infuriating. Those kinds of clichés should be taught in a fucking class or something! *Hear what's been said, people! It's a cliché for a reason! Warning! Warning!*

But no. It's just a small cliché people say backhandedly. It should be put on the sides of buildings with a skull and crossbones sign behind it.

"Steve?" I asked, not knowing what the fuck was going on and praying to *any God* that he was fucking joking. "What are you talking about?"

I was calm, but not really. I was the calm your mom is when you're in trouble. You know the kind. Like when your father is mad and freaking out like dads do, and it's like, "Oh, shit, Dad's mad," but when Mom's mad, she's all quiet and calm and it's like, "Holy fuckin' shit, Mom's mad." I was *that* kind of calm.

"My phone rang and I was driving, I didn't recognize the number so I let it go to voice mail and he left a message saying he's been watching me and if I know what's good for me, I'll stay away from you," he explained all in one breath.

"Do you still have the voice mail?"

"Yeah. Fuck, Leola, who *is* this guy? You said your husband's name is Matt," he complained as he dug out his phone.

"It is. Let me hear the message." And he put his phone on speaker so I could hear.

"Hello there. My name is Steve. You don't know me, but I know you. I'm calling to extend a friendly warning to you, and I'm hoping you'll accept it. Stay away from Leola. Take that as a warning or a threat, I really don't care. I'm watching. Stay away from her."

I looked up at Kaleb. *What the fuck was going on?*

"So who is he, Leola? What have you gotten me involved in?" he demanded.

I was dumbfounded. I couldn't believe this. Who the fuck did Steve think he was? I had underestimated him.

My phone beeped with a text just then. *Hello, beautiful.* It was Steve. *Whatcha up to? Anything new?*

My blood turned to ice, and I showed the text to Kaleb.

I looked out the windows in the back and went to the front door and looked out the peephole. I couldn't see anything out of place, but I didn't have a huge vantage point from inside my house. *Could Steve have followed Kaleb here?* I wondered.

"Fuck me, Leola, what the fuck!" Kaleb was clearly pissed. I was terrified. *He knows about Kaleb. He would tell Matt. Do I have to tell Matt?* Steve was crossing some serious lines. *Fuck fuck fuck!*

I paced back and forth between the kitchen and the living room.

Kaleb just stood there watching me. "What's going on! Tell me!"

I sat on the back of the couch and faced him. My phone beeped again. Another one from Steve. I opened it. *Would be a shame if Matt came home from work early today, wouldn't it?*

My heart stopped. My blood froze where it was. Kaleb was in my house and Steve knew it. We were trapped. Holy shit—Steve knew where I lived. My kids would be home from school that afternoon, and *he fucking knew where I lived!*

What do you want, Steve? I texted back.

I quickly explained the situation to Kaleb while I waited for Steve's reply. "But I don't know why he's gone so crazy. I've been as honest as I could with him. I didn't make him any promises!" I was shaking. What the *fuck* was I going to do now?

Another text came. *I want you, Leola. It's all I've ever wanted. You just don't know how to LISTEN!!!!!!*

And then my phone rang.

I screamed and dropped the phone. Shaking, I picked it up as Kaleb came around to help me. It was Ever. I answered it and she started to say, "Oh and one more thing—" but I started to yell at her.

"Ever! Please, I'll explain later, please pick the kids up at school and take them somewhere, not to your house, but somewhere public! Okay? *Okay?*" I yelled, the panic in my voice clear and intent.

"Yes, okay, I will! What's going on?" she yelled back.

"I'll explain later, I can't now. Please, Ever, please just do this! I'm afraid! Steve has lost it and I'm afraid. Please just do it!"

"Yes, I will. Don't worry about them. Call the police, Leola!"

"Yes. Yes, okay, I will. I'll be in touch." And I hung up.

My whole world came crashing down around me. Matt was going to find out about Kaleb. That was the worst part. I never wanted to hurt him. I just wanted to heal me. I cried and cried in frustration and anger. I felt myself getting red hot inside. I would kill this motherfucker before he ruined my life or hurt anyone I loved. Hatred spewed out of me like a gutted elephant.

"Okay," I began, "you take your car and I'll take mine. He can't follow us both. Let's go different ways and meet at …" My mind frantically searched the city for somewhere to go. I went into the kitchen and rummaged through drawers until I found a knife.

"What the fuck, Leola? You're going to kill him?" Kaleb demanded.

"Maybe!" I shot back. "Maybe! If I have to. This guy's gone crazy, Kaleb. He knows where I live. He's followed me, he's followed you—I have kids! I have my husband, my family, my life. If I have to, *yes, I will.*"

He watched me as I ran around for my purse and keys and phone. "Okay! So we're going to drive different ways and meet at the first condo we made love in. Do you remember it?" He nodded. "Okay, I'll meet you there. Here, take this." I handed him a knife but he put his hands up, not taking it. "*Take it!*" I shoved it at him. "Let's go."

We left the house together, and Kaleb quickly walked me to my car to make sure I got in safe, all the while looking around for anything suspicious. Finding nothing, he raced to his car, and we pulled out of the driveway one after the other.

Kaleb turned right and I turned left. Watching out my rear-view mirror, I didn't see any other vehicles on the road pull away after either of us. I turned the corner and sped to the condo, a fifteen-minute drive that felt like hours. I argued with myself whether to call Matt. I wanted to take care of this on my own. Exposing my affair with Kaleb had driven me to murderous intentions. I was afraid for myself and what I was capable of. I plugged in my Bluetooth, went to my Favorites, and pressed one of them. Steve answered on the first ring.

"Hello, beautiful." His voice dripped through the phone like putrid honey.

"Hello, hot stuff," I seethed. "What are you up to?"

"Oh, not much," he began. "Just out on a leisurely drive around the city. A nice day for a drive, don't you think?"

"Oh, yes," I squeezed out through clenched teeth. "Where are you going?"

"I don't know yet. I'm following a new friend. Perhaps you know him?" he teased.

My heart sank. *He's following Kaleb*, I thought. I needed to get to that condo before them. I ended the call and hit the gas. Hitting every red light (Murphy's Law!), I pulled into the condo's parking lot and saw Steve's car. On a quick scan as I ran I didn't see Kaleb's. *Shit motherfucker—they got there first!* I ran to the condo. When I got there, I stopped dead.

The door was ajar.

35

TERROR ROSE INSIDE ME. Every hair stood at attention, and I felt a heightened sense of awareness. I felt the wind on my arms, I smelled the exhaust from the street flanking the condo units, and I tasted the rush of blood as the adrenaline madly pumped through my body. I was aware of every eyelash as it changed direction slightly with each blink down the curve of my eye. I stared at the door handle, a flood of emotions, thoughts, and decisions shooting through me like a meteor shower crashing through my brain.

I simultaneously thought about calling the police, about whether my kids were going to be okay, whether to call Matt—what if this doesn't go well? I could be charged with murder. I could be murdered! I wanted to run and hide, and at that moment I felt my body responding, the flight instinct screaming through me.

But Kaleb was in there. Did he mean more to me than my life with my family? Was I willing to put my future at risk for him? I was incredulous as I stood there frozen in time as the realization pounded into me of how Blake's life and death had affected me, this small point in front of a door to someone's condo like the bottom of the funnel of a tornado beating the air above.

The eye of the storm was right here where I stood. And as the storm ripped at the sky and Dorothy's house spun above me, my blood started to boil at the undeniable truth that was my fragile heart.

I focused on the door handle again and closed my eyes. A sudden rush of sucking wind struck my face, and I opened my eyes and as I looked into Steve's face, I started to cry. I looked past him into the condo, but I didn't see Kaleb. "Where is he?" I demanded through my tears.

"Come in, sweetheart." Steve pulled my wrist and stepped to the side as he dragged me in. "You're just in time."

"Steve, please. What the fuck are you doing?" I felt the anger building inside me. *You fucking piece of shit, don't fuck with me.* "Where's Kaleb!" I spat.

Steve laughed. "*Kaleb*? Ha! Don't make me laugh. Don't you think I know what you're doing? You think you're so smart?" He walked around me, looking at me like I was an idiot. "Kaleb. Give me a fucking break. 'Kaleb' is not here."

I was confused. Didn't he say he was following someone? "I think there was some sort of car accident on the way here." My heart stopped. What was he talking about? "Something to do with a telephone pole, and oh—it was nasty. Going around a corner too fast, methinks. The guy must've been in a hurry."

The earth stopped moving. *It can't be.* Again! Not again. I couldn't speak. I couldn't move. Spots formed before me. I felt like I was going to faint.

"Too bad for him," Steve continued, an invisible cage forming as he walked around me. "A familiar story, Leola?" He was playing with my mind. Blake can't be dead again. Kaleb! *Stay in the here and now, Leola,* I silently demanded.

A familiar story? My eyes went to Steve, questioning. Out of the corner of my eye I saw Sanity sitting in the corner, tied up to a chair, watching me. Helpless.

"What—" I spoke, my voice deadened by an unacknowledged realization, venom dripping down the sides of my mouth.

"You have no idea who I am, do you? After all this time, you still don't recognize me," he said. Confusion coursed through my brain. "I had held on to hope all these months that you knew who I was and that's why you were with me. Why you came up to me and asked me to be with you. Because you'd realized your mistake all those years ago. Of course I had to put myself in the right place at the right time. You made it almost too easy on me, Leola. And for that, I'm torn between being thankful and disappointed. It's always more fun when there's a bit of a chase. But, oh well."

As I stood there, an obvious blank stare on my face, he stopped in front of me and held out his hand, as if for me to shake it in introduction. I left his hand there and looked at him. "Beck. Pleased to meet you," he said plainly.

Everything in my body dropped. I felt light but anchored to the floor, all the weight having dropped there like I was a helium balloon being held in place by a brick. Beck. *Holy fucking shit.* I saw my life flash backward before my mind's eye and rewind to before Blake. Beck, who'd gotten all weird with me in college and then suddenly dropped out of my life, I'd never given him a second thought. He was an acquaintance of Blake's. I remembered him being around here and there but never paid much attention after that awkward date. The guys at my parents' grocery store; the rude one who listened to the details of my life and then turned abruptly away. It was Beck.

Oh my fucking God. He's been watching me all these years. He came to the swinger's club to seduce me. How he'd felt familiar in my arms when I first met him. How he'd told me he loved me and always had. How he wasn't going to let me go "again." And Emma. "Emma," I said to him then.

He was smiling, clearly enjoying my jaunt down memory lane, watching as my face recognized points here and there and put the proverbial puzzle together. "Emma. Nice girl. I only needed her to get to you." He flashed another smile, in his glory. "She's none of your concern anymore, Leola. Nice pussy, though, eh?" He laughed quietly for a moment and looked down as if in respect. "She's gone," he said looking up at me. "I have no use for her anymore, haven't for a while. It's always been you, Leola. I don't know why you still can't understand that."

I felt my legs give way, and I reached for the couch to stable myself. "Matt?" I looked at him with pleading eyes.

"Matt's fine." He waved off my concern. "I don't want to hurt him if I don't have to, Leola. I need him to take the kids. We don't need kids where we're going, and I'm not a monster!" He chided me, like it was my idea to kill someone, as if I was some kind of heroin addict who needed fix after fix.

"As long as you do as you're told, no one else has to die. I think there's enough blood on your hands, don't you?" He held out his fingers, counting, "Blake, Emma, and now Kaleb," explaining to me as one would to a child who'd been bad and needed to know why she was being punished. He laughed. "You think I don't know what you were doing with Kaleb? The resemblance is uncanny, but I made sure you weren't with Blake back then, and you're not meant to be with him now!" He yelled in my face, forcing me to lean back to avoid getting spat on.

"*You killed Blake?*" I screamed. My heart ripped to shreds. I sobbed.

He was quiet for a moment, allowing me the dignity to break down one fiber at a time. *How kind.*

Sanity was fighting with the ropes in the corner, desperate to get to me, but I felt her weaken.

I suddenly remembered my knife. My hands clenched, the rage built inside me. All I could see was red. I locked eyes with sanity, and the connection and understanding was instant. The ropes immediately started breaking, and as sanity fought to get free to reach me, my breathing deepened and grew deliberate and I felt the fire and intensity build as I slowly straightened up.

Steve stood off to the side, waiting for the pathetic female to exhaust herself of her hormonal outburst, clearly bored with the wait. My heart was racing, every muscle in my body poised and ready to attack, and my teeth clenched. As the feeling built, sanity tagged me out and adrenaline took over.

Steve didn't even feel me coming.

And as I felt the knife go in to that soft spot over and over, pitting inch-long gashes where I blindly struck, I couldn't help but feel a little bit sad. Not just for me, but for other women in the future. Even though he was certifiably insane and it needed to be done, it was a real crime to see it go.

It really *was* the nicest penis I'd ever seen.

Thank you doesn't begin to express my gratitude to all those in my life who've helped me out with this book. I will begin with my husband Rob and my girls Simone, Viola & Adria who've graced me with countless uninterrupted hours to work on this novel. Thank you & I love you so much. I couldn't have done this without your love & encouragement. You are my heart & soul. And secondly thank you to my parents, Vince & Diane who, without your love, financial & otherwise, this book would still be filed away on my computer. Thank you so much to my brothers, Chris for your support & my brother Rob who captured amazing photos & took my vision in words for the book cover & executed it into reality with perfection. You are amazing. I want to thank Leola, your spirit will forever be captured here; I hope I did you justice in a fun story about a spunky woman who will live on in our hearts forever. I want to thank Mary K for proofreading this manuscript for me at the last minute & doing a wonderful job. And I want to thank my best girlfriends. You are my ground, my laughter, my cheerleaders & the loves of my life. ~DJKLMST~

Thank you to those that read my drafts & to all my family & friends for supporting me every step of the way. I love you all. I am truly blessed.   ~Jennifer~

CPSIA information can be obtained at www.ICGtesting.com
Printed in the USA
LVOW130845160613

338678LV00001B/22/P

9 781475 974232